T0128804

THE
CLANDESTINE
RUBY

James Glover

THE CLANDESTINE RUBY

iUniverse books may be ordered through booksellers or by contacting:

iUniverse
1663 Liberty Drive
Bloomington, IN 47403
www.iuniverse.com
1-800-Authors (1-800-288-4677)

ISBN: 978-1-5320-0592-3 (sc)
ISBN: 978-1-5320-0593-0 (e)

Library of Congress Control Number: 2016914204

Print information available on the last page.

iUniverse rev. date: 08/25/2016

This is written for my deceased mother, deceased wife and oldest daughter, my current wife, my son, daughter, and grand children

CHAPTER ONE

THIS WRITING IS THE SEQUEL to "The Gilded Web" written in 2011, where two college seniors, Jeremy McCuthchin,(white)and Rodney Blake(black) both very close friends, are on their way back to New York where they both live, after spending their summer vacation in Ft. Lauderdale before their graduation. This took place in 1980, in a time when racism was still very prominent and unfortunately tolerated by the majority of Americans!

On their way home in the middle of the night, deep in the south, they hit something that they assumed was an animal of some Kind but they never found the body because of the darkness, and decided to report it to the sheriff in the closest town before continuing on. This proved to be a big mistake because of the racial climate.

What they hit was a drunken hunter staying at a nearby hunting lodge, wandering off in the country side, and was later hit by another vehicle driven by the coroner's son and his friend, who were also drunk, living in the same town where the boys stopped to report their accident. When the coroner found out what had happened, from his son, he decided to pin the homicide on the two students in order to protect his son when the body was later discovered.

The coroner John Cuthbert is now sitting in his office at home, since his former office has been taken away, and is pondering the mistakes he made 6 month ago. John is around 58 years of age, five foot ten, 150 pounds, with light brown hair flecked with gray, with short white sideburns.

He is struggling with a mixture of regret and moral ambivalence. He has lost his license as a coroner and is on indefinite suspension by the board, but Harold has hired him as a part time investigator on criminal cases when they come up. The new coroner has also hired him as well as an on-call technician when needed. With his pension, social security benefits and savings, he is financially solvent for the time being. He and Toby have a distant, but mutual professional relationship and talk from time to time.

The town sheriff, Toby Reliford had befriended Rod and Jeremy because of their honesty, and decided to investigate the matter himself after vehicular homicide charges were filed against them. After tedious work and constant criticism from the locals, sheriff Reliford and his friend Attorney Harold Stienmetz, the prosecuting attorney in the case, eventually cleared the boys of the charges. Toby was a portly kind of man and walked with a confident gait. His hair was snow white and he appeared to be in his late fifties or early sixties. His face was round and friendly with crinkles at the corners of his eyes. He smoked a bulldog pipe, and his complexion was ruddy.

It is now 1981, a year later, on New Year's Eve, and Harold Stienmetz enters Toby's office to talk about the events of the recent past year, following the sensational trial and release of Jeremy and Rod, making them both local heroes in the small town, and in the neighboring black community across the rail road tracks.

"Howdy 'ol buddy," Harold greeted him, "still basking in all your glory?" he added with a broad grin covering his face. He was distinguished and well dressed, even in these late evening hours. He appeared to be around Toby's age, maybe a few years older. His hair was still a light brown, but was reluctantly giving in to flecks of gray. His face was unique with a small bird like nose. He was tall and thin, maybe six foot tall and a hundred and fifty pounds.

"Well, if it isn't my famous and highly esteemed friend!" Toby responded, getting up from his comfortable lazy boy with his pipe emitting a halo of sweet smelling tobacco. "What's the latest news in town?" he mused.

"It appears that we have started something, and it's a good thing," Harold responded, sitting down in the chair next to Toby's desk.

"And that is?" Toby quizzed.

"It appears that the blacks from across the way are now beginning to visit our town, and are taking part in a joint effort with the 4H club here and theirs as well. " Harold continued, with a smile, leaning back comfortably in his seat. "It appears that the sacrifices and total lack for your own safety during the upheaval there, has made you sort of a hero with them," Harold concluded.

"That was certainly one hell of mess wasn't it?," Toby responded.

"Well, it certainly accomplished what we had hoped it would, when it was revealed that the NAACP had sent in agents to uncover the racial steering practices by our realtors that keep blacks from buying homes here." Harold finished.

"Yeah" Toby continued, "especially after the KKK burned a cross in the yard of the home where the family lived who tried to buy a house here," Toby said taking a deep draw on his pipe as Harold leaned closer with excitement

"That was a smart strategy by the NAACP to do that, but nobody, including me, expected you to come under gunfire because you chose to come to the defense of the coloreds," He continued with obvious consternation.

"You certainly shocked me and everybody else here in town," he continued, "when you went into the black's area to break up the ensuing riot that took place," Harold said in admiration.

Toby leaned back in his chair staring whimsically into space as he recalled the experience. He felt that as sheriff, it was his responsibility to uphold the law for everyone involved, no matter the color or race. Toby reminded Harold that it was not just about him that things came out the way that they did, but that without his great and spectacular work as the trial attorney, it would not have happened.

Harold simply smiled with a nod.

Toby also recalled how important it was to Harold to have the work of the two boy's classmates from school to come down and help in the investigation by gathering facts in the case without drawing suspicion from the locals.

Just before Harold had come into his office, Toby was reading a letter from the fathers of the two boys they were talking about.

"I didn't mean to disrupt your reading," Harold said apologetically, noticing the letter that Toby was holding.

"No, that's perfectly OK," toby responded, taking off his reading glasses and concentrating on Harold. "It's just about a new private investigation agency that the two have just opened up together in the Bronx, and have asked me to come and run it for them," Toby concluded.

"Now that their sons have graduated with their degrees, both have expressed a desire to work as investigators in the agency if I take the job. The agency will also be complete with a forensic laboratory for Ralph to continue his DNA work there. He's planning on giving up his graduate work with the FBI to join us," Toby finished.

Harold emitted a noisy whistle of surprise and disbelief, with raised and arched eyebrows. Things like this just don't happen in this small town of 595 people. The silence in the room was deafening for a brief moment.

"Whew," that's amazing he uttered.

"Yes it is," replied Toby, "and a complete shock as well."

"What are you going to do?" continued Harold's inquiry.

"I really don't know. I haven't mentioned it to Peg yet."

"Yeah," said Harold, "but it has to be exciting and tempting."

"I can't lie," Toby responded in wonder. "I've worked as a sheriff for over twenty years here and there, but to run a private investigation agency in a big upstate location is really kind of surreal and a little overwhelming to think about," he said wide eyed.

"Man, this sounds like a fairy tale straight out of Disneyland, "Harold mused. "This is extremely exciting. I'm very glad for you"

Both men laughed at Harold's remark, nodding their heads in agreement. After Harold leaves the office, Toby sits quietly now in the dark, puffing contently on his pipe, enjoying the pungent aroma from it and contemplating what he would tell Peg. There was no doubt that he wanted to take the job offer, but knew that it would entail a lot of difficulty, especially now that he was so popular and loved here in Midway and in the black community.

He was not overly concerned about Peg's acceptance of him taking another job, but of the total relocation and moving from the south to upstate New York. That would be total culture shock, neither of whom having ever left the south nor having lived in a large metropolitan area. This time he was not so sure that Peg would not have an opinion one way or the other.

The night was still young and darkness blanketed the small town like a velvet cloak as Toby climbed into his car and began the drive home. The silence was broken only by the sound of crickets and the humming of his car. This stillness and calm would be one of the things that he knew would be missed if he and Peg did move to the big city, with its busy streets and never ending noise and traffic jams. They had gotten spoiled with the laid back and unhurried life of rural country living.

As he neared home his mind traveled back twenty years ago when he and Peg first moved to Midway after leaving Atlanta where he served as sheriff. They had just put both of their two children through college and were now ready for Toby to become his own boss. Pulling into the driveway of his home, a nice but modest one-story brick ranch, he thought how nice it felt being sheriff here in spite of dealing with the prejudice mindset of a small southern town.

As he neared his driveway, he could smell the succulent odor of his favorite meal, roast beef, baked potatoes, collard greens and cornbread filling the air. Peg certainly was the world's best cook, and he had told her so numerous times. It was a wonder that he stayed as slim as he did, when other men his age had begun to get fat bellies. Entering the front door, he was greeted with a kiss and a smile.

"Well, welcome home stranger," Peg said. "I thought you'd be home earlier."

"I would have if Harold had not stopped by to chat," was Toby's reply. He took off his shirt as he talked and made his way to the dining table, noticing the casual way that Peg's blouse had slid down her shoulder, revealing half of one of her ample breasts. She was mid 50's in age, medium length blonde hair and blue eyes. Her short skirt barely came down to her knees. She always had nice long shapely legs, and was still quite a dish after all these years Toby thought.

"No way," Peg told him, noticing the way he was looking at her. "There will be none of that before dinner." Toby just smiled and sat down at the table.

"What did Harold want when he stopped by?" Peg asked.

"Nothing in particular, he just wanted to talk about the condition of things in the town. When he noticed that I was reading a letter he apologized for interrupting me before he left."

"What letter was that … anything important?" Peg asked curiously.

She noticed his body language and the expression on his face and quickly added, "If you'd rather wait until after dinner that's perfectly OK." She concluded.

Toby inhaled deeply and let out a noisy sigh. This was as good a time as any, he decided because waiting would not make it any easier.

"It was a letter that came yesterday" he began "from the fathers of the two boys, Rod and Jeremy, offering me a job in the Bronx, to come to New York and head up a new private investigation agency that the two of them recently opened together in the Bronx"

"What? You're kidding," was Peg's unbelieving response. "**New York** and a private detective agency?" she repeated again in utter amazement.

"That's right,"

Peg was at a total loss for words as she struggled to digest what her husband had just told her. Toby knew what she was going through because that was exactly his initial reaction when he read the letter. Very seldom in their years of their marriage were both of them at a loss for words at the same time. Toby's mind was racing trying to figure out where he would go next. This was every bit as difficult as he imagined it would be.

"According to the letter, they were both very impressed with the police work that I did with their son's cases, and could find no better person to head up agency but me."

"Since it's a new enterprise, have they considered any other person?" Peg asked.

Toby "I don't know, the letter made no mention of any other prospects"

Toby had an uneasy feeling in the pit of his stomach at Peg's question. It came too early in the discussion, which Toby felt was due to some kind of uneasiness with Peg.

"That question makes me think that you are not comfortable with the letter."

"Well, that's right to a degree. It's not just the letter but all the implications involved."

Like what?" Toby pressed on, knowing that this was a crucial point in their conversation. He wanted Peg to completely state her case. He noticed that she squirmed uncomfortably in her seat for just a moment, but quickly gathered herself.

"There's no doubt that you have earned the right to have something like this happen to you. You have always worked hard and sometimes with little or no reward, like being appreciated or being paid as you deserved. That's not my concern."

"Then what is," Toby asked in earnest.

"Moving to New York is not like moving to Midway from Atlanta. It's a completely different ball game. We've lived here in the south all of our lives in relatively small quiet places, other than Atlanta which you were glad when we moved from there to come here, 'too big and noisy' you said. But even I know that Atlanta will be nothing compared to the Bronx, New York. That's a huge, busy place, Toby. Are you sure that's what you want?"

"It's not just what I want, but what you want as well." Toby responds. "Let me continue," he tells Peg. "The pay will be nothing like the small salary I earn here, I assure you. The detectives that I will have on staff are the college classmates of Rod and Jeremy, who have all graduated from Wayne State and will come and work for the agency only if I accept the job. Ralph will have a complete forensic lab in the office as well, to conduct his DNA testing and work, just like he did during the investigation for the boys last year."

"You make it awfully hard to argue against the terms of the job offer," Peg replied, "but it's more than just the job," she continued. "What about the people here and your work for them as sheriff?"

"I admit that is a major concern for me, one that I have thought about very seriously," he admitted.

"This is that once in a lifetime opportunity that is talked about,' the fork in the road experience.' It may not come again." He concluded.

"I know you're right," Peg conceded.

"I'll set up a meeting with the town leaders tomorrow in the town hall and let them know of my decision to take the job," Toby said reluctantly, "Then I'll plan to go to the black community as well once that is done."

"Even though this is very intimidating and nerve wracking, I'm in favor of your decision and will go wherever and whenever you're ready." Peg responded.

Toby reached over and pulled her close to him in a warm and tender embrace. This why he loved her so much as he did. She was always in favor of what was in his best interest, and never complained, even when he decided to leave Atlanta which was a decent paying job on the police force there, to take the job offer in Midway as sheriff, in order to be his own boss with less pay. Before going to sleep, he and Peg made love together to seal the deal and bring about a sense of closure.

Early the next morning, Toby headed to his office for an early meeting with deputy Bivens, a tall, slender man in his early thirty's with a large Adams Apple and big hands. After a hot cup of coffee, the two sat down at his desk and began their conversation.

"Willie Joe," Toby began, "I know you've grown up a lot in the past year, especially in race relations, after what happened here recently. I have a lot of confidence and trust in you now that I didn't have before."

"Sherriff, I think that you have something that you want to say to me," Willie Joe surmised, seeing the expression on Toby's face, tone of his voice, and the unexpected vote of confidence he had just received.

"You're right, I do," Toby confessed. "I want to make you my replacement as sheriff when I leave to go to New York and take a job there."

"**Whoa,** back up one sheriff! Run that by me again, Willie Joe said in total shock.

Toby smiled faintly at his deputy's response. "I have been offered a job in New York to run a brand new private investigation agency formed jointly by the fathers of the two boys that we cleared last year"

"You're joking of course."

"No, I'm dead serious," Toby answered with a somber face. "I've already talked it over with Peg, and she is in total support of my decision."

"Wow," was all that Willie Joe could utter.

"I will talk with the town hall leaders and tell them of my recommendation to have you replace me, instead of going through the whole reelection process. I want you to take care of the office today while I get busy calling everybody."

"You got it," the deputy replied, hitching up his pants and sticking out his chest proudly.

Toby busied himself making one phone call after another. While he did so, he smiled at the way that Willie Joe was conducting himself as interim sheriff. Other than the usual amount of phone calls, nothing out of the ordinary occurred. Telling the committee of his decision would not be too difficult as he was certain that he would get their full approval. It was telling the community about leaving that would be his biggest challenge.

At the end of the day, Toby went home, and he and Peg called their children to tell them, and each one of them congratulated their parents. After dinner, both went out to the front porch and settled comfortably on the couch, while the soft gentle night breeze caressed their cheeks.

"You know, we'll miss nights like this when we leave," Toby said almost thinking aloud.

"I know," Peg responded, "I was just thinking the exact same thing."

It's really strange how when two peoples have been together for a long time, they begin to look and think like each other, Toby thought, smiling.

Early the next morning, Toby is meeting with the board in the town hall, while Willie Joe runs his office for him.

"Gentlemen," Toby begins, "I've asked you all to this special meeting, to tell you of a very important decision that I have made with my wife's approval. "I have been offered a job in upstate New York to head up a new private investigation agency located in the Bronx."

You could literally hear a pin drop in the room. Each one of the men looked at each in stunned silence and disbelief. "When did this take place?" one of them asked Toby.

"Only yesterday," Toby replied. "The fathers of the Rodney and Jeremy, the two boys who were on trial here last year, are the ones who made me the offer."

"This is a shock, but comes as no surprise, considering how well you managed everything," one said.

"Where does this leave us exactly" another asked.

"I have thought long and hard about that," Toby began. "I would like to make a recommendation for your consideration"

"And what is that?" another asked.

"That my deputy Mr. Bivens, take over the duties as sheriff after I'm gone. His work has been excellent, and I can think of no better person to replace me."

"This is an unusual request, Toby," another of the board said. "However, we trust your judgement."

"This would save us all a lot of trouble not having to hold another election to replace me, which won't produce anyone more capable than Willie Joe." Toby concludes.

Toby is asked to leave the room as the board talks over his recommendation, and will be asked to return once a decision has been reached. Toby agrees and goes back to his office to wait for their call. Upon his arrival, Willie Joe informs him that Mr. Elliot, an elderly gentleman in his 90's has just died.

"I can't leave the office until I receive word from the board," Toby tells him. "You'll have to take care of it and make all of the arrangements with the family and the funeral home."

"I'm on it," his deputy said, putting on his jacket and standing up to leave.

"Oh, by the way, I recommended you to replace me to the board."

Geeze," Willie Joe remarked, "I'm honored.

After a half hour or so, Toby was asked to rejoin the meeting. He entered the room with some trepidation not ever having this experience before. He still remained confident however, and was reasonably relaxed. He was informed that the board had decided to honor his request, but that their decision would still have to meet the approval of the community at large.

"How will that be done?" Toby asked.

"Well, we were hoping that you could provide us with a plan," the moderator replied.

Toby was not expecting to be put in this position and had no immediate answer.

"Let me sleep on it," he responded.

"Take your time," another member responded. "By the way, when is all of this to happen?"

"I don't know exactly," was Toby's response. "They are willing to wait until the agency is staffed, and I've made my final decision." As for a plan, I intend to call a meeting of all the citizens to break the news of my leaving. Maybe that would be the best time to get their approval."

"Excellent idea," came one response. "Well, I guess this concludes our meeting," he continued. I want to thank everybody for coming, the meeting is adjourned."

Toby exhaled deeply. Another task done, he breathed, relaxing. There remained only two things left to do; call the two fathers and tell them of his decision to take the job, and that everything is all set, and he is now ready to go whenever they call, and secondly, get all the people together for his announcement.

"How'd everything go at the office?" Peg asked him when he got home that evening.

"Better than expected. We got all of our business taken care of, my request was approved, and all I have to do now," he tells Peg," is call New York, and get the people of Midway and the black community together."

"You certainly have taken the bull by the horns," Peg responded enthusiastically.

Toby then called John McCutchin and James Blake in the Bronx to tell them of his decision. John answered the phone.

After listening to Toby's message about accepting the job and being ready to go, John rubbed his hands briskly together with a broad grin. John was well groomed and meticulous in his dress. His suit was Tailor made and fit him like a glove. He was at least six feet tall and slender. His medium length hair was light brown and he was in his fifties. He worked as part time banker and Wall Street broker.

James Blake was soon heard joining the conversation with an excited voice and greeted Toby warmly. His voice was very heavy and his speech was articulate. His complexion was a medium a brown, his mustache was well trimmed and jet black, like the color of his well cropped black hair. He was also well dressed in a tailored suit and around fifty years old as well. He worked as a very successful business consultant and manufacturing executive.

After John fills James in with the details of Toby's message, the three exchanged enthusiastic conversation about where to go next.

"All we have to do now is get the ball rolling," James added.

"We'd like for you to come as soon as you can" john tells Toby.

"I have a town meeting scheduled in two days to meet with the people here in Midway," Toby said, "and then Peg and I will be ready to leave."

"James and I have already made accommodations for the two of you at our best hotel, until final arrangements are completed on your home." John concluded.

"Once you call us when you're ready, we'll schedule your flight itinerary," James informed him.

Toby was given the address of his home in the Bronx and directions how to get there once they arrive. As far as he was concerned, there was nothing else to be done, Toby concluded.

He then had the head of the 4H club to issue a notice to all the people of Midway and the colored section across the tracks as well, to come to the town meeting to meet with him.

The town hall was packed! There was standing room only, and the buzz in the area was a low roar with anticipation, as everyone speculated about the nature of the meeting. Nothing like was done since the calamity of last year's rioting.

Toby stepped forward on the platform to the roar of the people, and waived his hand to quiet the hubbub of the gathering. The blacks and whites intermingled together, and this pleased Toby very much.

"I know you're all wondering why I called this meeting," he said to the now hushed crowd.

"I don't really know where to begin so I'll just start anywhere. Peg and I will be leaving Midway very shortly. I have been offered a new job in New York, and I've accepted."

All of a sudden you couldn't hear yourself think over the noise that erupted. People waved their hands in disbelief, and began talking to one another instantly. The noise was like a low roar.

When Toby was finally able to quiet the crowd, one of them shouted out when was this going to take place, and another wanted to know just where this leaves them.

He began by saying "I know you all have a million questions to ask, and I'll try my best to answer them, but first let me say that I understand your being shocked by this, because I was too when offered the job the other day."

"Who offered you this job?" someone wanted to know.

"You all remember the two boys that were on trial here last year?" he asked them.

All heads nodded in remembrance.

"Well, the boys fathers went together to form a new private investigation agency in the Bronx New York, a little over a year ago right after their sons graduated from college, and asked me to run it for them."

The crowd was silent for a while, but the noise from the busy minds at work could be heard for miles. Toby waited for more questions to come from the crowd, determining that it would be much easier to answer their questions instead of trying to explain everything himself.

Finally a black person someone broke the silence, "Sheriff, where is this going to leave us? We in the colored section across the tracks have come to depend on you to fend for us in critical times."

Toby was glad that this issue hit the floor. He wanted to know how the black community felt, and whether or not they would be free to talk about this in Midway. He breathed a sigh of relief.

"I don't think that will be an area of concern," he responded. "Deputy Bivens, my replacement, has vowed to carry on the relationship between the coloreds and the folks here in Midway. Nothing will ever take us back to the way it was before."

There was a smattering of applause from the crowd, and gestures of appreciation from the people, visible by handshakes and smiles.

"When are you leaving, Sheriff?" another person asked.

I don't know exactly," Toby answered, "I have to notify them in New York whenever I've finished up my business here. There's one unfinished piece of business that must be taken care of, however," he continued. "I have made a recommendation to the board to name my deputy, Willie Joe Bivens as my replacement. They have agreed to honor my request, but that is dependent upon your final approval as well."

Again there was silence.

Someone broke the silence by saying to Toby, "If that is your recommendation and it's been approved already, then I don't see the need to carry this on any further."

There was total agreement by everyone in attendance by voice acclamation.

"You know how difficult this is for us. You're the best sheriff we've ever had here, bar none. But we all realize at the same time, what a good opportunity this is for you and Peg. We've come to love both of you, but we're not going to be selfish. Just let us know when you hear anything. We know that we can depend on deputy Bivens to carry on."

Those words were spoken by the moderator of the board, and effectively closed out the meeting. There were handshakes, hugs and tears galore, as Toby and Peg exchanged good byes to everyone present. Peg was overwhelmed with tears of sadness and relief that everything was finally over.

Back in his office for the final time, Toby called New York, and John McCutchin answered the phone. "Toby, is that you?"

"Yeah, it' me, John"

"Man, it's good to hear from you. Hold on for a second, John said," I need to get James on the line."

There was a momentary silence on the other end of the line, then an audible click.

"Hey man," James said apparently excited. "We've been anxiously waiting for your call. How'd it go for you there?"

"Excellent. Everything went perfect. No problems at all."

"Good," Toby heard John say. What's our next move?" Toby asked.

"We are in the final phase of getting your apartment ready," James tells him. "We just need another day or two."

"I need you to get a pen and some paper to write down the following information" John directs him.

"OK," Toby responded, as he put down the phone and got a pen and paper from his desk.

"Al right, I'm ready"

John gives Toby the address of his apartment, and the directions of how to get there.

"It's in the high rent district where it's safe and quiet in the suburbs. We have a lot of crime here in the Bronx as it everywhere else, so we chose you a nice safe place to live. Peg will love it. It's a little expensive, but we'll take care of that."

"I'll make your airline reservations as soon as you give me the word," James said.

"Word," was Toby's remark, with a broad grin.

"We'll look for both of you in the next several days. We'll call you back when everything is all set," John concluded.

Toby sat back in his chair, took out his big bull dog shaped pipe, filled it chock full of his fragrant tobacco, lit it to a glowing ember, and took a big puff. As Willie Joe watched him, he knew that the sheriff had received good news.

"Tell you what I want you to do, Willie Joe," he said. "Spread the news that Peg and I are leaving for New York this weekend."

He nodded, and suggested to Toby that it would be good if He wrote a prepared statement to the town folk, thanking them for all of the love and support they've given over the years, so that he could read it to them when he broke the news.

Toby was in full agreement, and commented what a splendid and thoughtful idea that was that Willie Joe had made, as a big plume of good smelling tobacco rose to the ceiling, fumigating the entire room. Toby was at complete peace at the moment, relishing the wonderful feeling that washed over him. IT WAS FINALLY OVER! OVER, he sighed heavily.

Meanwhile in New York, Rod and Jeremy has just received the word from their fathers that Toby had accepted the job offer and would be headed for the new office in a few days.

"I'm so glad that Toby decided to come up," Rod said. "I would not have been interested working for the private detective agency if he had not accepted the job to be our boss."

"My sentiments exactly," echoed Jeremy.

"Their corporation had received a number of requests by affiliated businesses, according to dad, to investigate looking into establishing a private detective agency to meet a growing need in the area, while furthering to diversify the scope of their Winfield Enterprise, they formed together over two years ago" he finished.

"It's ironic, isn't it, that right after they opened up the detective agency, a huge robbery took place here in town, at a prestigious jewelry store, and the police have yet to recover one missing item, a valuable ruby worth $30,000 dollars. Everything else was recovered, and the criminals were soon apprehended, but the store owner insists that the ruby be found and returned, which has now been missing for several weeks." Rod added.

"Until that happens, the police cannot close the case. It's unfortunate, because they did an outstanding job with everything else. Since they did not have the manpower or the time to pursue only one missing item, Lt. Bob McNichols suggested that the owner hire our agency to find the missing ruby." Jeremy said.

"And that's what he did." Rod acknowledged.

"After we graduated from Wayne State, and the Winfield enterprise had agreed to follow the suggestion to diversify, I was shocked to be asked to work with Toby, if he accepted the job, as his investigator." Rod replied.

"Yep, me too" echoed Jeremy.

"It was really nice to know that Ralph would also be working with us, it's just like old times" Jeremy said.

"This arrangement will work out great, especially since we already work for them in the corporation, and don't have to worry about money coming in to support our families, when the agency does not have enough work for all of us and Toby too, it works out perfectly, Rod concluded.

CHAPTER TWO

TOBY AND PEG BOTH LOVED to fly, but dreaded the trip to the airport with all of the hustle and bustle that goes on there, as well the hassle of boarding times, finding the right corridor, not missing their flight time, paying the high price for food, baggage check ins and retrieval, as well as the hassle of changing planes and lay overs. These were things that they were not used to and could very well do without. But flying was a sign of the times and something that must be endured.

Toby loved the exhilarating feeling of leaving the ground, and looking down as the earth gradually became smaller as the plane gained altitude making houses look like toys, and the cars traveling over the roads reduced to specks. He always chose a seat next to the window where the wing was so that he could observe the movement of the flaps that controlled the ascent and descent of the plane. This way he could see any malfunctions that might occur.

This was the result of a couple of problems that he had experienced while flying when in the military on their cargo planes when getting few hops to go home on leaves. He was told that what good would it do to see if anything goes wrong because it wouldn't do any good or change things? While he knew this to be true, he could never forget the reality that he was never really "flying", but instead were experiencing controlled "free fall".

None the less, he was fascinated by the experience. It made him aware of how helpless he was off of the ground, and of the words that he had often heard said "there were no atheists in the air."

Peg sat quietly next to him reading a book, while other passengers either were listening to music on their head phone or watching a movie being played on the movie screen. He surmised that this was their way of keeping their minds off of the very same thoughts that crossed his mind.

Luckily their flight was nonstop to New York. They exited upon arrival, retrieved their luggage at the baggage claim center and proceeded to the exit where they would be picked up. "Not too bad after all" Toby said to himself, as John and James picked them up in a luxurious black limousine.

"How was the flight?" John asked as they settled comfortably in the lush padded seat.

"It was not as complicated as I thought it would be." Peg answered obviously glad that it was over. "Well, everything is all ready for the two of you," James added. "We're on our way to your apartment."

Toby and Peg were speechless as they looked at their apartment wide eyed. They had never lived in a place that was this expensive looking in their lives.

The apartment was set in a very upbeat suburban neighborhood, with a spacious green lawn which was well manicured. The building looked almost new, and was finished with what looked like real cobble stone brick. The front door was oversized, and trimmed in beige, to offset the rustic colored stucco finish.

The inside interior was being painted with basic white, and was very spacious, yet still intimate. It contained two baths and a luxurious master bedroom, with a spacious walk in closet and a full bath complete with a Jacuzzi.

"Nothing but the best for our director" John said. "We are extremely happy that you accepted the job, and we want to make you and Peg as comfortable as we can."

"From our perspective, you have certainly outdone yourselves," Peg responded.

"Oh, by the way, Peg, you will have to do some shopping with our secretary as soon as you are ready to buy furniture for the apartment, because it's unfurnished. This was like news from heaven Peg thought to herself. "We have you booked into a hotel to stay until you've finished shopping". James told her.k

"We know you're tired and want to rest," John told them, "So get you a good night's sleep after dinner. We want to take you to the restaurant of your choice. What's your favorite?" He asked them. After discussing this between themselves, Peg and Toby decide on Chinese food.

"We have a busy day ahead of us tomorrow" James informed them "We want to introduce the two of you to our staff, the families of Rod and Jeremy, and the rest of our executives."

Toby was excited with anticipation, but a little jittery at the thought of it all. He had never been feted like this before. After dinner, Peg and Toby settled into their apartment, both trying to relive the events of the past twenty four hours which seemed to have passed like a blur.

"Can you believe this," Toby asked Peg. "This is all so unbelievable, almost surreal."

"Yes. It's like that for me too," Peg acknowledged. "I hope the bubble doesn't burst" she added whimsically.

Toby was in full agreement with her sentiments. This new job would mean no more wearing uniforms of any kind, police or sheriff. He relished the thought of wearing just a suit and tie to work. This would be a first for him and was like a dream come true.

"I can't wait until tomorrow, "Toby exclaimed like a child with a new toy. "Let's celebrate" he said to Peg with a lustful eye. Toby undressed her slowly, savoring the still sexy fullness of her ample breasts, and buttocks. They made passionate and intense love, leaving no stone unturned. Peg had two incredible orgasms, soaking Toby with her juices. The two completely collapsed in each other's arms, and almost instantly fell asleep.

The next day began with a big breakfast and the subsequent trip to the office with James and John.

"Let me show you the car you will be driving," John told him when they arrived at the headquarters. "It comes with a liberal travel allowance" he concluded. The car was a new midsized white one, parked outside the headquarters building. Toby commented how much he liked it. Peg nodded her agreement. Once inside, they were greeted by Jeremy, Rod and their families. Toby was amazed at how much the two boys had grown and matured in just a year. He was close to tears when they both rushed over to hug and embrace him. Peg looked on in wonderment.

"You will never know how much this means to us, "gushed Jeremy as he shook Toby's hand. Rod and Ralph were in full agreement and equally happy as well. Tears moistened the eyes of the boys as Peg fought back tears of her own. John and James were equally as overcome with joy and gratitude.

"We owe this all to you, Toby" James said. "If it wasn't for you and your belief in our boys when they were framed, we don't know what would have happened."

"Of course as you can see, they are no longer our boys, but grown men and college graduates along with Ralph" John commented.

Toby just gawked as he looked at both of them. They looked the same, just more mature. It's amazing how the transformation happened, he thought to himself. It's almost magical he mused. Jeremy was now 22 years of age, but his frame was still wiry and lithe, but had now become very muscular and filled out. He still had the same rugged handsomeness, but a more matured face. His eyebrows were a heavy dark brown, framed by locks of sandy colored hair. He was around six feet tall and Toby guessed his weight to be about one hundred and eighty pounds.

Rod was the spitting image of his father, James, but taller. His body was still very athletic looking and muscular, like the college running back that he was. His hands were big and powerful, and his black hair was cut very short. His mustache was neatly trimmed and his shirt showed off his physique. He looked the same as he did in Midway, only a year older.

"Both Rod and Jeremy are now married to Beth and Andrea, who is now two months pregnant. Jeremy and Beth won't be too far behind them according to Jeremy," John finished.

Toby looked across the room to where the two girls were standing. How beautiful they had grown to be, Toby thought. Somehow it seemed that girls matured much more noticeably than boys. After talking with Rod and Jeremy for a brief period, he signaled to Beth to join him. She was not the same blonde, blue eyed girl with the long pony tail he remembered. She was now a full bosomed woman with a figure to make other women jealous.

He wanted first of all to know how her mother and father were doing ever since they found out that her brother was involved in the cover up of Rod and Jeremy being framed.

"They've accepted it and have moved on," she responded.

Have you ever forgiven your brother for punching you in the face when you confronted him for being involved in the cover up?"

"Yeah, it's OK. Mom wanted me to tell you that she is sorry for the way that she treated you, when you tried to tell her about everything, and how she accused you of trying to sabotage our family."

"Well, I understood how she felt, Toby responded. "It's hard to accept sometimes, when a family member is implicated in a criminal investigation, and trying to protect her daughter from her brother when you acted as a sheriff."

Beth acknowledged Toby's explanation by holding his hand affectionately.

"How did she feel about you and Jeremy getting married since he was a northerner and an outsider?"

"Once he was cleared, she was OK with it. The hardest part for her was my moving away."

"How's your brother doing now? He asked her.

"He's doing all right. He no longer has anything to do with the Coroner's son and his friends, and has apologized for hitting me. He knows now how wrong he was."

"All's well that ends well" Toby said. They ended their conversation with a warm embrace and Toby then waived to Rod to rejoin him. He said to him that he was not surprise in the least about him and Andrea getting married. He could see it happening even while the trial and investigation were going on. Then they rejoined the crowd. By now the room was noisy with conversation going on all at once.

After a short while, John and James returned, and informed the crowd that they and the boys were going into the conference room for a business meeting, and that they were free to continue with their gathering. Once inside the conference room, Toby exhaled deeply at the size and décor of the room. It was filled with a large circular table and expensively covered chairs. Don't these two ever have a limit on the amount of money they spend Toby wondered? He asked them this very question.

James with his deep voice said "Of course we have limits, but the Corporation that we have formed, WINFIELD ENTERPRISES, is very substantial."

"The name of your private detective agency is **Reliford Investigations**, of course. As the name implies, you will be the man in total control of the whole operation as its sole, full time private investigator, and will be responsible for everything, including its financial solvency. That means that it will be up to you to balance the budget of agency every year, and to find new clients on an ongoing basis. Our corporation will have your back only when needed, but will not interfere in the daily operations of your agency" John said.

"As you can see, this is the reason that we called on you for this job. We need someone with your experience and expertise to handle the job" James finished.

Toby's heart was racing, and he feared that the beat of it could be heard around the room. Not in his wildest dreams had he ever imagined having a business named after him, let alone being in charge of it. John's voice cut into his thoughts and yanked him back to reality. His palms were sweating profusely, and he hoped his feelings were not too obvious.

"We have a net worth of over 30 million, and the financial support of several other firms that we do business with, John added. Our corporation will take care of your salary and those of your employees when they are assigned to you. This includes your agency's expenses, travel allowance and your housing.

It's a package that we're sure you and Peg will find very comfortable."

"This will be a very fluid operation involving both Reliford Investigations and Winfield Enterprises. By fluid we mean that there will be an intimate relationship between your company and ours. When you need to add other investigators other than yourself, Winfield will supply them. Jeremy, Rod, Dick and Ralph all work for Winfield full time, and will be loaned to you in certain cases like this one." James said.

"Jeremy works for my investment firm "John said. "Rod works for his father's consulting firm. Ralph works for one of our subsidiaries; Crescent Chemicals, as a chemical engineer, and Dick works as an undercover detective with the police force. All four of them have asked to be assigned to you as your investigators whenever you need them, like now. When they are on loan to you, we will take care of their salaries."

"Toby, this will be a very demanding job for you, and being the only full time private investigator, you will stay busy handling the caseloads that come your way alone. Besides finding the missing Heirloom ruby, there are two other clients that are waiting your services as well." John added.

Toby nodded his head knowingly.

"Do you have any questions about anything you've heard so far?" James asked.

"Nothing that I can think of except our client and how soon they want our agency to get started" Toby answered.

"That's what we wanted to hear," John replied, rubbing his hands briskly together. "Here's where we are so far. Our client is Monsero's Jewelry, a Jewish owned store, and one of the area's largest and most esteemed shops. The president Is Gary Smith, he's the one who called us. He has an Heirloom ruby worth thirty thousand dollars that is still missing, and he wants it found more than anything else. Even though there are some pieces still missing, he is confident that most of it will be covered by his insurance.

"Well," James began, "The police have recovered most of the missing jewelry that was stolen, but the owner is only concerned about the missing Heirloom ruby. The thieves in custody claim to know nothing about the missing items anyway, let alone any talk about a missing ruby. When asked concerning its whereabouts, they all claimed to know nothing, even after successful Lie Detector examinations. The police do not have the time or the man power to look for the one missing item that the owner is requesting with no supporting evidence of its existence."

"So that's why he hired us?" Toby asked.

"Correct," John added. "The item is priceless to him, far beyond just the amount it's worth, but he's not saying why."

"The police were completely stymied at first about the robbery. They had nothing to go on. No clues were left at all. "They felt it this was carried out by highly trained professionals, and that the heist was very well thought out and planned down to the smallest detail. No windows or doors were broken into, no internal alarms were set off, and there were no finger prints left, only some blurred photos from the store's hidden cameras. They had never encountered anything like it. This is why Mr. Smith called us." John added.

"Whew," Toby exhaled, "It sounds as though we certainly have our work cut out for us."

"The police know that we are on the case, and are more than willing to work with us in any way that they can. If you need to contact someone on the police force for any additional information or help, ask for Lt. McNicols. He's a friend of ours and our contact."

"Well, there you have it in a nutshell. "Do you have any question that you have to ask us that we haven't covered?" James concluded.

"Nothing that I can think of?" was Toby's response.

"Then I think it's time to have your staff come in and be brought up to date on where we are," John said. James stood up and headed for the door when John finished, and motioned for Jeremy, Rod, Dick and Ralph to join them.

Ralph Simon, like both Rod and Jeremy had matured well. His studious demeanor and appearance suited him well. His hair was a dark brown and thick and curly, and he had a manicured moustache. His face was framed with expensive black rimmed glasses. He was of average height and weight

Dick Wingate was very different in stature and looks. He was much taller and his hair was blonde, long and thinner. He was clean shaven in a fresh scrubbed kind of way. He had a rather boyish looking face still, like a choir boy. His manner was less studious and reserved.

When they were all seated around the conference table, they were ready to begin.

"As you all know by now, Toby will be your new boss. Not me or James, but Toby. He is the only one that you will answer to. Of course, James and I are always ready if you need us," said John.

All four of the investigators nodded in understanding. Once more James and John repeated what they had informed Toby previously.

"Let's get you all over to your building so that we can get started with our investigation." John advised, as they all stood up and got ready to leave. When they arrived at their agency, words could not express Toby's reaction.

John and James led them to their company vehicles parked outside. Toby and his staff climbed into the staff car while James and John rode in the corporate marked vehicle. Once they arrived at their destination, the executives handed Toby the keys to the office and left them with goodbyes.

There on the sign in front of the office building were the words RELIFORD PRIVATE INVESTIGATIONS. Wait until Peg sees this was his first reaction, he thought to himself. This was like a dream come true.

Once inside, he was very impressed with the interior layout. They entered into a gathering room where coats and hats were to be hung before going into the main office. The office was divided into two parts. The first was the office reserved for the investigators which had a round table, with five chairs, a large filing cabinet and a blackboard centered in the middle of the room. The second section, divided by a portable wall was the Toby's office, and in the back section of the room was the secretary's office desk.

All four men took seats in the investigation room, seated in a semicircle.

"Well Guys, what do you think?"

"This is absolutely fantastic" Jeremy gushed. The other three nodded their heads in total agreement.

"You will never know how glad I am having the four of you as my investigators" Toby told them. Ralph, your work during the investigation last year as our microbiologist and forensic expert was outstanding. So was your work as our chief detective and investigator," he said to Dick.

"We owe you two a boatload of thanks," Rod said to them. "If you hadn't come down from school to help us, I don't know what would have happened. The circumstantial evidence against us was overwhelming. Attorney Steinmetz would have been up the creek without the information that the two of you gathered up for him to defend us."

Toby agreed with a nod of his head. "Before the two of you came down, I was not very optimistic about the outcome of a trial by jury. Nobody in Midway knew any of you and you all were outsiders from up north as well. The deck was certainly stacked against you."

Toby then told the four of them how glad he was to have them as his investigators.

"All of the work that you do for me will be paid by the corporation on a weekly basis the same as mine. All of you have living expenses that your salaries should take care of since this will be your full time job.

"Dick, I hope this is good news to you since you have opted to work for me instead of the FBI." He said to Wingate.

"No problem" was his reply.

"There are two company cars available for each of you to share as needed. When you finish using them, make sure that the gas gauge is full. You all have a gasoline credit card which I will issue to you, and I will monitor them closely to ensure that we stay within budget. ID badges will be ready tomorrow for each of you, to present only for identification purposes when asked. They will not be worn on your clothing, for much of what you do will be undercover. Any questions thus far?"

"What are our working hours, and when do we report for work?" Jeremy asked.

"Be here for work at 9:00 in the morning ready for work. It is now 3PM and time for me to let you go home, while I call Lt. McNicols to bring us completely up to date. We will have to go to police headquarters in order for the meeting."

"Police headquarters?" said Rod, "This gets more exciting by the minute."

"You said it," Dick exclaimed.

"See you all in the morning," Toby said as he dismissed them.

Once they were gone, Toby went to his desk, called Lt. McNicols at police headquarters and scheduled the meeting with him for 10:00 in the morning. He then slumped down in his oversized executive chair with its expensive leather upholstering, and pulled out his big bulldog pipe, a package of his aromatic tobacco, and smoked it in complete leisure, filling his office with its fragrant aroma. He reviewed the information that he gave his detectives to see if there was anything that he left out. The boys had no questions when he asked them, so he must have covered everything.

On his way to the apartment, he couldn't wait to tell Peg about the events of the day. He was sure that she would be in from her shopping spree. He stopped at a Chinese restaurant on his way to the apartment and got a takeout order for their dinner. He knew that Peg couldn't wait to get her own stove to cook on. Both of them were not crazy about eating food brought home.

When he entered the door, Peg greeted him before he was able to close it. She was all excited. Toby couldn't remember her being this excited, since she told him that she was pregnant with their first child. She was like a child with a new toy. Toby let her speak first. Peg was all excited because she had never experienced seeing so many shops and stores to browse in and buy the items that she wanted. She could have bought her furnishings at one of a dozen stores.

"I know that you will love the colors and styles that I picked out for the apartment," she gushed excitedly. Toby let her finish before telling her about his experience with the corporate headquarters, and his private investigation office with HIS name on it. He told her about his meeting with his investigators and their appointment in the morning at police headquarters.

"This has certainly been some kind of a day," Peg exclaimed.

"It certainly has," Toby replied. "Now let's get some sleep, we've got a busy day tomorrow."

At the office the following morning, Toby and the three investigators meet in the investigation office before their trip to the police station.

"When we meet with Lt. McNichols, he will explain in detail about the investigation, the arrests, and any other pertinent information. Feel free to ask him any questions that you might have" Toby informs them.

When they arrive at police headquarters, security guards meet them at the front gate.

"Can I help you," one of them asked Toby.

"We're from the Reliford private investigation agency, here to see Lt. McNichols," Toby tells him.

"Wait here until I call him" the guard replies.

The four waited for seemed like an eternity before the guard returned. "I need for you to sign these papers," he tells

Toby handing him the forms. "Lt. McNichos will be out for you shortly."

After a short while, the Lt. appears in full uniform. His appearance was striking. His uniform, obviously tailored, fit him like a set of Marine Corp dress blues. He was tall and thin but well built. His hair was short and well groomed. He had a very thin but well mustache, short mustache and clean shaven face. He looked like a military drill instructor.

"Well, here are my special guests this morning," he says to the guards, "Escort them to my office and I'll join you there in a minute."

All of the guards immediately nodded their heads and led them inside. Dick was especially impressed, as were the others.

"Sort of reminded you a little of the FBI, did it not" Toby mused as he watched him. Dick smiled faintly. They were then led to the McNicol's office, where they were seated in the waiting room. Ralph commented about how attractive his secretary was.

"Still the playboy" Jeremy teased him. The all laughed at his remark. With that Lt.McNichols entered the room.

"Mr. Blake and Mr. McCutchin told me about you. Welcome," he said shaking each of their hands. "We're glad to have you helping us on this case. Have a seat here, gentlemen," he instructs them as they gather around a table arranged in a semicircle.

"I personally am happy to have you all joining us in this investigation, and hopefully with your help we can officially bring this case to a final closure, or until the insurance company of Montero's settle the claim with them. Since the owner, Mr. Smith insists that the ruby is unaccounted for and therefore we cannot officially close the case, even though all the other items stolen have been recovered. As far as the police's role is concerned, our investigative work is done."

"If the thieves claim to have no knowledge of the ruby, and have passed lie detector tests to prove they didn't, then how do we know that there really is one?" asked Ralph.

"Good question," Bob responded. "It is listed on his inventory at 30,000 dollars, and no one including the thieves, know anything about it."

"Whew," whistled Rodney. "Why would he have something worth that much in his store to begin with?"

"This is what his own insurance company asked him as well" he answered. "They are reluctant to pay this amount until they have reliable information to substantiate the claim."

"That's exactly what we asked him also," James volunteered.

"He said that he had an offer from a buyer an intended to sell it after celebrating his thirtieth anniversary with his wife in order to put his grandchildren through college. The buyer was considering buying it before the break in." John said.

"Our role, then, is simply to find out if the Heirloom ruby even exists, and if it does, to find it?" Toby stated.

"That's right" remarked Bob. "By the way, all of you can refer to me as Bob from now on. We are a team."

"Then I'm Toby, this is Dick Wingate, this is Jeremy McCutchin, and this is Rodney Blake." Toby concluded pointing out each one.

"Very good," Bob tells them, "let me begin from the beginning." He said, pushing back in his chair and let out a big breath. "Feel free to stop me at any point if you have questions."

They all nodded their agreement.

"When we first began the investigation, we had no clues whatsoever, we were baffled. There were no fingerprints left behind by the thieves, there were no forced break in's in any of the windows or doors, and no interior alarms were set off. We had never encountered anything like this before. It was a very professional job, not just an ordinary one."

"Then how did you know to respond?" asked Dick.

"When they stole everything they wanted, they simply opened the front door and left. That's what set off the alarm to notify us." Bob explained. It was only during the interrogation of the perps later after they were apprehended, did we learn how they did it and what their MO was."

"Who were they?" Rod asked highly impressed with the work of the thieves.

"I can't wait to hear this," Toby said, leaning forward with his elbows on the table and his hands under his chin.

"Me too," exclaimed Dick in wonder, joined in turn by each of the others. Bob observed them carefully with a faint smile.

"We learned that all four of them had served time in prison for various types of crimes including robbery. Unfortunately, when criminals spend time in prison, one of two things will happen. They are either rehabilitated, or become more determine not to make the same mistakes again that got them caught." Bob said.

"That's too bad" Ralph responded "But unfortunately it's a fact of life."

"In this particular case, the four of them met while serving their time, and got together to form a coalition, sort of like a brotherhood of thieves. Unfortunately, as luck would have it, they all lived relatively close to one another. This enabled them to get together and map out their crime at the jewelry store"

"Like Ralph was saying, it's a shame that that kind of ingenuity could not be used for constructive purposes.

"You can say that again" echoed Jeremy.

"In this case, the thieves gained entrance to the jewelry store by cutting through its ceiling ventilation system after the shop had closed, and after the entire building itself was also closed. The building's HVAC system covered the whole structure."

"Obviously they must have staked out the area thoroughly in advance." Dick observed.

"You're absolutely correct, as you will see later" Bob acknowledged.

"They began by gaining information about the building's layout from the traveling agency next to the jewelry store. They used fake work order ID's at the travel agency, using work clothes and a pickup truck outside with a fake company name, claiming to do an annual inspection of the HVAC system. They waited until the clerk inside had several customers that he was working with, before approaching him. The clerk signed the order forms they handed him, to begin their work in the utility room.

"They were banking on human error which thieves often do," Dick commented.

"You're absolutely right about that! Toby, I can see already that you have a good staff to work with you." Bob commented.

They poured laboriously over the layout, taking notes and drawing exact details of the system.

4 men entered the building, but only 3 left after their work was supposedly finished. The clerk was busy and failed to notice."

"I'm glad you noticed," Toby said with a grin.

"The man left behind, crawled through the overhead ventilation shaft in the utility room, taking careful pains to replace the cover after getting inside. While waiting for the building to close, the thief in the ventilation system smoked nervously as he edged his way toward the jewelry store next door. This proved to be his undoing."

"How so?" asked Rod.

"Well, of course you all know that there is no such thing as a perfect crime."

"Everyone nodded their heads in agreement.

"The thieves all smoked while the robbery took place, becoming too complacent with their work. This became their ultimate downfall. After the interrogation of the four was concluded following the arrest, we matched the DNA on the cigarette butts left on the floor, with the butts they smoked in the interrogation room afterwards.

Ralph was beside himself when this was revealed, because it brought to mind so vividly about his previous work in Midway to free Rod and Jeremy from their frame up, how he was able to determine through DNA, the difference between the human blood, planted on the boy's car by the coroner, from the animal blood that was originally on their car from the accident.

"I knew that Ralph would get a big charge out of that" mused Toby, "He knows his stuff."

This brought a chorus of laughter from the other two and a smile from Bob.

"The thieves gained entrance to the jewelry store, when they entered the ventilation shaft by cutting through the ceiling, disarming the alarm systemto the outside in order to let his buddies in. It was only natural for our detectives to check out the shaft thoroughly."

"Once inside the building, the thieves took their time looking at all the cases of jewelry they were interested in, before breaking into the cases to gather up all of the jewelry, knowing that once broken, the alarm would go off. So they took their jolly good time looking. This is where their complacency got the best of them. They were so confident in what they had accomplished, that they failed to wear masks to disguise themselves." Bob concluded.

"How did you apprehend them?" Rod asked.

"When we received information from the FBI about the identity of the thieved from the photographs that we sent them, we found the stolen items in each of their houses that we got from the FBI."

"That sounds a little strange that they would keep all of the stolen jewelry in their own homes" Rod commented.

We wondered about that too," Bob confessed. "We discovered later, that they did not trust each other enough to keep the stolen jewelry hidden in their hideout out, for fear that one of them might sneak back and steal more of it."

"So even though they could depend on each on each other to pull off the heist, when it came to the money, all bets were off," Jeremy commented.

"That's right," Bob observed, "When it comes to money, you can't trust anyone."

"Are there any more questions that any of you might have about anything we've talked about so far?"

"I have a question," Dick said. "What happened to the stolen jewelry that was recovered?"

"After we gathered everything together, we turned it all over to Mr. Smith at Monteros, in order for him to check it all against his inventory, to make sure that it was all there."

"And then what?" Rod asked.

"We allowed him to keep the jewelry until everything was checked out by his insurance company."

"When was it all given back to him to keep?" Jeremy asked.

"Right after the OK from his insurance company it was all returned to him for keeps."

After a brief a brief pause without any more questions, Bob continued by directing his comments more to Toby than anyone else.

"As you can see, we have come to the end of our rope in this investigation. Everything from here on in will depend on you and your agency. Rest assured that we will be at your disposal at any time to render any assistance that you might need."

Toby thanked Bob for sharing everything with them. There were handshakes of appreciation all around the room at the conclusion of the meeting. It was now painfully clear what the task of his agency was. After leaving, Toby and his detectives headed back to their office, where he immediately made a detailed report to James and John of their meeting with Bob. The two were very impressed to say the least, and left the remainder of the case to them.

"Let us know when you are ready to start in order for us to begin to pay your salaries, and to provide anything else." John said

"Oh, by the way, I forgot to tell you. My secretary informed me that Peg has finished her shopping and has everything she needs for the apartment, and the painters have finished their work. You can move into the apartment at any time." He said.

"We will inform Mr. Smith that you will be contacting him from here on out, and that your agency will proceed with everything ASAP." James said.

After James and John left the building leaving Toby and his crew alone, Toby addresses the group.

"Well fellows," Toby told his staff, "This is where we begin the new chapter of our lives together as Reliford investigations. It's up to us now to solve this crime."

"Where do we begin?" Jeremy asked.

"First I've got to go to corporate headquarters and get your ID badges in order to get started, then we'll get together again for final preparations. We'll actually start tomorrow morning at nine."

After Toby and his crew ended their meeting, he headed home to talk with Peg about everything that has happened. It was all unfolding so fast that he needed to just unwind and relax. Needless to say, Peg was ecstatic about moving into her apartment.

They're going to be delivering the new furniture tomorrow, and we'll be moving in. I know that you are glad about that. Finally, I'll have my own kitchen, No more eating out every day" she concluded.

"I know that's right," Toby remarked. He summarized his day to Peg, including the meeting at the police station, his time with James and John, and the plans to begin their work with his investigators first thing in the morning.

"You know, all of this is enough to make you dizzy with disbelief. Here we have our own upscale apartment in the suburbs with new furniture, and me and my crew will begin the first day of Reliford Investigations in the morning. Can you believe it all?" Toby said in wonderment.

"It's all is a little hard to digest all at once," Peg agrees.

Tomorrow will be the first day of the rest of their lives, and they can't wait.

CHAPTER THREE

E ARLY THE NEXT MORNING, ROD, Jeremy, and Ralph meet with Toby in the investigation room of the agency to discuss where they go from here. At the onset, their secretary comes into the room with the ID badges for each investigator with a knock on the door. Her figure that did not escape Ralph's Eagle Eye, and her dark brown brunet hair spilled over her shoulder.

"Good Lord in heaven," he muttered softly to the others, "If God had something better, he kept it for himself."

All four of them laughed, causing the secretary to wonder what was going on.

"Oh it's only a private joke," Ralph replied, winking at her. "My name is Ralph, and these are my associates, Rod, Jeremy, and Dick, and our boss Toby Reliford."

"Thanks for the introductions," Toby said to Ralph. "You'll have to excuse him."

The secretary introduces herself as Trudy, and says that she is glad to be working for them.

"Not near as glad as we are," Ralph concludes with a wink. After the secretary is gone, Toby tells the investigators that it is now to get down to serious business.

"I have no secret master plan of where we begin" he tells his staff. "What we should do, is explore every avenue that we feel the police did not explore during their investigation. From what I can deduce, they examined every shred of evidence at the crime scene, including cigarette butts, camera photographs which ultimately led to arrest of the perps, and the recovery of the jewelry, the DNA of the butts left at the scene and the interrogation room, so what does that leave us?"

"Not much at all," Dick replies. "What do you suggest?" he asked Toby.

"Well, first of all, I would recommend that the four of you canvass the surrounding area, and talk to everyone in the vicinity of the crime, to see if anyone has any information that the police failed to look for during their investigation. You never know what might turn up. As for me, I'm going to the store and have a talk with the owner. The missing ruby is supposedly valued at fifty thousand dollars, yet to recover it, the owner is willing to hire a private investigation agency to get it back, which could end up costing him much more. He must have a hell of a good reason."

All of his investigators agree.

"Does anyone have any questions or other opinions?"

There was nothing.

"Then let's get started," Toby directs.

Ralph, Jeremy and Rod begin their work under Toby's supervision. All three agree to begin their work by talking to the store's security guard.

"He could have simply been overlooked initially, by the police during their investigation." Dick suggested.

"You could be right," Rod added, "Especially with the concentration on trying to figure out the MO of the thieves, and scurrying around to get any information they could, with the scant amount of evidence that they had to work with. Anyway, since the security guard was off duty at the time, there would be no reason question him."

They were in complete agreement about that being their first priority.

Loading up in one of their company vehicles, the three headed for the jewelry store.

"May I help you," a woman's voice said as they entered the shop.

"Yes you may," Jeremy said," We are from here from Reliford private investigations, to speak with your security officer."

"Just a moment," she told them, "I have to tell Mr. Smith that you're here." She said as she walked away and disappeared through a door. In a few moments, she reappeared with the owner, a middle aged man with thinning white hair, and very neatly dressed. He was of average height and weight and his face clean shaven.

'Gentlemen," he greeted them, shaking each one of their hands..

"Mr. Smith, I assume," Jeremy said.

"That's right. Toby called and said that he would stop by later. I am sure glad that you all are on the case. I won't delay you. I'll get my security guard in here right away.

He turned to his secretary and told her to get the guard, and then left the room abruptly. In matter of seconds, the secretary returned with the guard. He was youngish, maybe around 35 or so, small in stature and size. He shook each of the investigators hands.

"I'm Tod Fletcher, the security guard here at Monsero's", he said introducing himself.

"The pleasure's ours," Jeremy responded. This is Rod, Dick and Ralph, he said introducing his partners.

"We're here from Reliford Investigations to talk to you about the recent robbery here" Dick said.

The guard acknowledge each one, and then invites them to join them in his office, directing the secretary to bring them coffee. The investigators were impressed with the professional way in which he handled himself. Once in his office, they were all seated at a desk, with small uncomfortable chairs. It was a far cry from theirs. The room was small and cramped, but adequate enough for what he needed.

"This is indeed a pleasure," he began. "You guys are the first ones to talk to me about anything, and that includes my own boss."

"Why hasn't Mr. Smith talked to you?" Rod asked.

"Probably for the same reason the police didn't. I was not here when the robbery took place. I leave at five. Still I thought that they could have at least talked to me" he said with a look of disdain on his face.

"Be that as it may, you are the security guard here, and you certainly deserve that common courtesy" Dick said.

That brought a smile and a look of appreciation to the officer's face. He thanked Dick for his remark.

The guard was obviously flattered by the boy's attention, and responded that he did his own investigation on his own.

"Did you find anything unusual that maybe the police had overlooked? Dick asked.'

"Not really," was his reply. "They did a real professional job with the robbery. I did not look tor anything in the store, because the police were very thorough in their investigation."

"That may be true," Dick responded, "But sometimes you have to think outside of the box when a crime is committed. You should never leave any stone unturned."

"That was my sentiment exactly."

"What did you do in your own investigation? Rod asked.

"I concentrated my search outside of the building, and on the grounds."

"Did you uncover anything? Jeremy asked.

"I did discover a very expensive brand of cigar butts in the alley behind the store the next morning after the police were finished."

"What was unusual about cigar butts?" Ralph asked.

"Well, I smoke cigars myself, and these were not the type of butts that the average smoker would smoke. They are very expensive and not sold in many stores," he replied.

Can you show us exactly where you found them? Jeremy asked.

"Sure" the guard answered taking them to the spot where the cigar butts were found. Some more butts were found still lying on the ground.

"Whoever was here was here for quite some time," Dick observed.

"You're right," the guard observed, "I just retrieved a few of them, just for my own satisfaction."

"This is very helpful information," Dick responded. "You have just given us an additional lead that we didn't have before. This is very crucial information for us."

The officer smiled broadly, even though he did not fully understand just how his information was so valuable. Once inside the office again, Dick asked if they could have the cigar butts that were left on the ground.

"Sure" the officer said. "Help yourselves."

"If this information proves to be valuable, you will certainly get the respect and appreciation not only from us, but from the police department as well," Jeremy told him.

"Ralph, go outside and gather up what you need to take back to the office." Dick said.

Just then the secretary stuck here head in the door to inform the group that Toby had arrived to talk with Mr. Smith. The boys thanked the security officer, and left the building to return to their office with a sense of euphoria and anticipation. This was a significant find. Back at their office, they gathered in the investigation room to discuss their next strategy.

Ralph, you're in charge of the evidence from this point on. Do whatever you need to do with it in your lab. The rest of us will determine what our next moves are from here," Dick directs.

"What this tells us," Dick stated, "Is that there is possibly a fifth man connected to this case, one that nobody knows about except maybe the thieves."

"If he sat outside of the store while it was being robbed, then that would explain why there was no photo of him along with the other four." Rod surmised.

"Exactly," Dick added." It would be my guess that he was the getaway driver."

"But why aren't the other four saying anything about this guy, if he is indeed connected? Jeremy wondered.

"Yeah, that doesn't make any sense" Rod said.

"Well, I learned in criminology class, that thieves, believe it or not, have a code of ethics among themselves. They don't snitch on each other."

"In many ways, they are more loyal to each other than most people are. Many people are backbiters. Remember the song that the OJ's sang about backstabbers." Rod reminded them

That brought a chorus of chuckles from the others.

"But seriously, we have a real, live suspect here that clearly deserves our attention. The security guard said when he showed us where the cigar butts were, that he patrols the grounds outside of the store daily as just a routine part of his job. He discovered them the day after the robbery." Dick summarized.

"That can only mean that he must have been there in the alley all along." Jeremy observed.

"Right" Dick acknowledged.

"Then where do we go from here. What's our next strategy?"

"It's obvious" Dick says. "A lot of times, there's often someone who notices these kinds of things." Dick said. "We need to canvass the entire neighborhood in the vicinity, to see if we can find someone who may have seen something. Jeremy, you check around the immediate area, and Rod, you canvass the houses for a couple more blocks."

They all agreed that since Dick was the trained criminologist, he should be the one in charge of the investigational proceedings. As they were concluding their meeting, Toby came into the building, and the secretary informed them that he wanted them in his office. The secretary made coffee for each one and took them into Toby's office, where they all thanked her and expressed their appreciation.

"Well, how'd it go today on your first investigation?" Toby asked them.

They all started to talk at once, and Toby reminded them that he first wanted his report from Dick, whom he says was in charge of investigations, and then wanted to hear from the others.

"We decided earlier among ourselves, that I should be in charge of the investigations." he told Toby. Toby smiled broadly, and told them that he was very pleased that they could police their own activities.

Dick brought Toby up to date on the proceedings of the day with the meeting with security guard.

"That sounds like you all made significant progress in the case. Just what I was hoping you would do. This changes everything. My meeting with Smith the owner of the store was OK, but left me with mixed emotions, which I will talk about at a later date." Toby told them. Just at that time, Ralph entered the room and joined the proceeding. They all took turns bringing him up to date on their findings. He tells them that his DNA analysis was complete, and filed away for future reference when needed.

"I need to call James and John, and give them this vital information. They will then relay it to Bob at police headquarters." Toby tells them. "I want all of you to go home, celebrate the happenings of today with your loved ones, and be back here at nine in the morning."

Once they were gone, Toby phoned Bob at headquarters and shared the information with him. He was ecstatic!

"This certainly changes the entire scope of things. We now suspect that a fifth person is a part of this whole process, but as of now we have no concrete evidence. We don't want the other prisoners in custody to know that we have this information. That would cause us to lose our element of surprise."

"I agree," Toby replied. "They already know who it is, and may tip him off if they suspect that we know. This is our ace in the hole. We will certainly keep you up to date on our progress."

"Good," Bob replied, "I knew that we made the right choice in choosing James and John to work with your agency."

"I'll call them as soon as we finish talking, and let them know that you and I have talked." Toby tells him. After they conclude their conversation, he calls the corporate headquarters and shares the information with John and James.

"Fantastic, simply fantastic," they responded. "Just let us know if there's anything that we can do," John said. Toby assured them that they were fine.

He could not wait to get to the apartment, and eat Peg's first home cooked meal since they arrived in New York. He was certain that she was full of excitement with her new furniture there as well. What an evening this would be for them. How right he was! This was like a New Year's celebration. They partied into the wee hours of the morning, until he reminded Peg that he was a working man, with four people to supervise each day for the first time, rather than just a deputy, and a committee that only met once a month like it was in Midway.

Peg told him before they went to bed, how impressed she was seeing him dressed in a suit and tie.

"You look like Matlock on TV." They both laughed together as they retired, exhausted, but happy.

Dick began his search by going from door to door in the immediate vicinity of the jewelry store, questioning the residents about any information they could or would share about the robbery, after showing them his ID, and stating that their agency was following up the investigation after being detained by the jewelry store owner to recover a valuable missing piece that was dear to him.

Many were a little irritated and reluctant to share much information with him, citing that the police had already asked many of the same questions.

"I understand why this would be a little frustrating for you," he told one person that he was talking to, "We just want to make sure that nothing was overlooked during the police's investigation."

"Well, you seem to be a nice young man," the old lady that he was talking to said, "And since this is for the kind man at the store, "I'll tell you everything that I know. I saw a car leaving near the scene right after everything happened, just before the police arrived. I didn't see much because it was getting dark, but I could make out the make and model of it, but not the color.

"Why didn't you tell this to the police?" he asked her.

"Because I didn't think it was important. I only saw the image of a car on the street without any details to describe," she added.

"Well, I certainly appreciate what you just told me," Dick said, "It might prove to be useful." He thanked the little old lady before he left, and made a note of this as he sat in his car. Immediately he thought that this could be a valuable piece of information, especially with the cigar butts that the store's security guard found in the alley. Just knowing the type of vehicle was important without any other details available, because that was certainly something to keep a lookout for.

Jeremy meanwhile was checking all of the stores in the area for any sales of this particular kind of cigar brand that might have been sold recently.

"You don't have to look far for this type of cigar," he was told by one store owner, "Most of us don't even carry it because it's so expensive, and most people here can't afford it. There are only a dozen stores in the whole city where this type is sold."

Jeremy was glad that his search had been narrowed. Rod had little or no success to report in his canvassing of people in the rest of the area, most of them refusing to cooperate, feeling that it was too redundant following the police's investigation. At first he felt that it was because he was black, until talking with the other guys, he discovered that they experienced much of the same.

After gathering all of their information, the three investigators met in the investigation area with Toby, to share what they had with him. Toby wrote each one's report on the blackboard in the center of the room, discussing the particulars of each.

"Each one of you, have given me valuable information. I'm very impressed with your findings.

"Dick, your information about the vague description of the vehicle seen leaving the area may be very significant. You were able to get information that was not given to the police. That was a good piece of human relations, and may prove to be significant in our investigation, and will help us in identifying the getaway away car."

"Jeremy, your work with the department stores in the area, will eventually bear good fruit I'm certain. That information will prove to be decisive in determining the identification of the person waiting in the alley.

"Ralph, once the identification of the fifth man, the getaway driver is known, you can then get a definite make on him from the DNA evidence that you have found.

"Rod, you just keep chopping wood, you never know what just might crawl out from under a rock."

Toby then turns his attention to the blackboard in the middle of the room to write down the results of their investigation..

"Let's see just where we are right now. First of all, the only real clue that we have are the cigar butts found in the alley behind the store, but with no suspect." He writes this on the board. "The second thing that we have is only a vague description of a vehicle outside of the store with no description. Am I missing anything?" he asked his crew.

"Anything else anybody wants to add to the list?" he asks again.

No one had any comments.

"This is a good start for the first day of work. Now I want to talk to all of you about my meeting with Mr. Smith the store owner. He has left me with mixed emotions and feelings of uneasiness. He seems like a good man, but some unanswered questions plague me. He has this missing Heirloom ruby valued at fifty thousand dollars still missing, but is willing to hire a private investigation agency to recover it, which may end up costing him much more than that."

"What was his response to that?" Jeremy asked.

"Only that it was that important to him. A family keepsake," he said."

"Why would he have something that expensive in his shop in the first place? Jeremy asked.

"The only answer he gave me was that he was holding it for an auctioneer who made him an offer to buy it. He intended to use the money to put his grandson through college."

"That's all and good," Dick replied. "But why hire a private investigation firm to find it, when you have insurance to cover it?"

"Good question," Toby answered. "It seems as though the insurance company is refusing to cover the cost, initially, because no one seems to know anything about the missing ruby, including the thieves, which the police also shared with them. Its existence is only on his list of missing items which have all been recovered."

"Then they seem to be wondering about some of the same things that we are" said Rod.

"Exactly," Toby answered. "He explained that until all of this cleared up, he wants us to find it for him."

"I see why you are uneasy with his answer." Jeremy said. "With his income and position, the cost of a college education should not be of much concern to him. There must be another reason."

"And that is exactly what troubles me" Toby said.

"So where does this leave us?" Rod asked.

"Up the creek without a paddle," said Toby. "I'll continue to concentrate on Mr. Smith, while the rest of you keep doing the work that you're doing. Something eventually will eventually turn up" Toby tells them. "Get an early start in the morning, and continue to canvass the area, and report to me in the afternoon when you finish." He added, leaving the writing from the meeting on the blackboard.

Toby decides to follow up on his analysis of Mr. Smith's books because of the lingering questions plaguing him. The next day, Toby pays him a visit.

"Mr. Smith, I need to take a look at your records for myself on behalf of my agency. AT this juncture of our investigation, everyone and all things are suspects, even the person that you purchased the ruby from. How do we know that he was not the one who stole the ruby? After all it's worth a small fortune. We are not about to leave any stone unturned."

"That's fine, Toby, after all I did hire you to do this job."

Toby then takes the time to review the jeweler's books. After a brief review, he closes the book and continues to question the owner.

"Let me first ask you some questions about you what you told me earlier that still troubles me. When I asked you what you intended to do with the ruby once we found it, you told me that it would be used to put you grandson through college."

"That's right."

"According to what I saw, you certainly have adequate financial resources to handle that without much trouble."

"Well, at first sight, that may seem to be the case, but remember I am responsible to pay your organization for your work, and also to have enough money for my retirement. I don't have an IRA or retirement fund like other working folk."

"That's true," Toby concedes, but why then are you willing to risk so much money to find the ruby, which may end up costing you more than the thirty thousand that the ruby is worth?"

"It's for a very special reason. I want to give it to my wife on our fiftieth wedding anniversary."

"Sounds like a noble gesture. Tell me why you have two separate insurance policies for your valuables?"

"One of course is for the missing ruby, and the other is for a valuable diamond that I keep in my safety deposit box in the bank."

"I suspect that that is the reason why you can afford our services among other things, your grandson's college education excluded."

"That's right."

"Why did I see two separate checks written for twenty five thousand dollars each?"

"One was for the ruby and the other for the diamond."

"OK, that ends my questioning for now. Thanks for your cooperation."

"Thank you for being so thorough in your investigation."

Toby left momentarily satisfied, yet still a little uneasy.

Early the next morning, Jeremy visits one of the department stores close to the jewelry store and asks to speak with the manager. When the manager appears, Jeremy introduces himself, shows him his business card and ID badge.

"Our firm is doing a follow up investigation on the behalf of Mr. Smith, the owner of the jewelry store that was recently robbed" Jeremy told him.

"Oh, yeah," the manager said, "I remember that well. How can I help you?"

Jeremy goes in his pocket and pulls out the wrapper of the cigar box that he got from the security guard, and shows it to the manager.

"We'd like to know if you've recently sold this brand of cigars to anyone."

"We don't sell many of these because they cost so much, and most are sold to business men and dignitaries. It shouldn't be much trouble getting that information if we have it. "Normally, we don't make it a habit of keeping records of sales, but some items like these we keep track of, because we order so few of them. Besides us, there is only one other store that sells these."

"If it's not too much trouble, I'd like to know the name of the other store as well" Jeremy tells him.

"Sure thing, just give me a few minutes," replies the owner, who then goes into another room near the back of the store.

After several minutes, the manager returns with a piece of paper in his hand.

"Here is a list of persons who brought this brand of cigars in the last month. Since they're so hard to get, we have their names and address' in to order to notify them when more come in." he said handing the list to Jeremy along with the address of the other store.

"I really appreciate this very much," Jeremy tells him with a firm handshake before leaving. At the other store, he had no such luck. They kept no records, and only reordered when they ran out. Jeremy felt very fortunate for going to the right store.

Later that afternoon, all four investigators report to Toby in the office.

"Well, how'd it go yesterday?" he greeted them with a smile.

"I drew a blank," Rod said first, "Nothing. Most of the people I talked to treated the robbery like old news," he finished, with his slumped shoulders and a dejected look on his face.

"Same here," said Dick, echoed by Ralph also.

Jeremy's heart was racing as he gave his report to Toby which contained ten names of persons who had recently purchased the cigars in question.

"This is great news, Jeremy" beamed Toby, as he looked at the 10 names written on the paper. The first thing that he did, however, was to cheer up the other three investigators who didn't have the same kind of luck.

"Doing investigative work is more failing than succeeding, believe me I know" he told them. "For every nugget you find, you find a bunch of rocks first. It's not like the glamorous life that you see on TV shows. Most of it is dull, routine work.

Get used to it. I'm extremely proud of all of you, because you carried out the assignments that I asked for. Jeremy was very fortunate to get these ten names of people who purchased the cigars that that the security guard gave us, because most retail stores do not keep such a good record system of **names** like these," he said holding up the list of names for the others to see.

"This does not mean that Jeremy's work was done any better than the rest of what you all did. Let's get that straight from the start." His words were like magic to the other three, causing their body language and countenance to change immediately. They all took turns congratulating Jeremy

"Before it's all said and done, each one of you will have contributed immensely to our investigation, believe me. However, be that as it may, this is fantastic news." Toby then turns his attention to the blackboard in the center of the room which contained the information of the progress so far in the investigation.

He points to what is written down.

"So far, all we have up to this point, is only **one** solid lead, the cigar butts found in the alley and nothing more. We also have one possible clue to examine further, the vague description of a vehicle seen on the street following the crime. That's it, other than what we have now from Jeremy, a list of ten names of men who have purchased these cigars."

He adds these names to the only other real solid leads; the cigar butts and now the list of customers who purchased them.

"Is there anything else that we might have missed?" he asked the others. There was no response, other than the negative shaking of their heads.

"Well, here's where we go from here. I want the families of each one of these persons listed to be examined in depth, along with the persons listed. I want to know their family structure, family health problems that might be hereditary or current, deaths in the family, and information like this." He finished.

"How in the world will be able to get all of this kind of information?" one of them asked. Dick raised his hand to speak, and Toby allows him to do so.

"We have to somehow go undercover" he said.

"Right Exactly" Toby replied enthusiastically. "Undercover!"

"What kind of Under Cover work do you have in mind, exactly" asked Rod, his heart racing with excitement and anticipation, as were all of the others.

"I want you to pose as marketing consultants for the cigar maker, Community Health Care investigators for the county, looking for preventive health care issues and family genetic traits, such as high blood pressure, heart problems, diabetes, etc."

"How will we be able to do this?" Rod asked.

"We will have to furnish each of you with fake ID's for each kind of assignment, along with the fake names of the companies you are supposed to represent. Corporate headquarters will furnish everything. First, you will pose as consultants for the cigar maker, verifying the names of the persons who actually purchased the cigar in question. Next, you will investigate the family history of each one, and the last thing will be the family's health issues. This is where Ralph will handle most of the work with his knowledge of genetics and DNA."

"Wow," was the overall response from the investigators.

"Now, now this is what I'm talking about!" exclaimed Rod excitedly. He was joined with the same kind of enthusiasm from the others.

"Each of you will be given three names in the initial investigation as consultants for the cigar maker, and you will report to me when you finish. Any questions?" he asked them. There were none.

"That's it for now. Go home and wait for further instructions. The Corporation has a lot of work to do. If any one of you need me for any reason, call my cell phone and leave me a message because I need to get busy on other cases that are waiting for me."

Toby now calls John and James to share the progress of the investigation up to this point. James answers the phone.

"James this is Toby. Got a minute or two?"

"Sure do" James responded. "John is out on business and won't be back for a while, but let's talk. I'll bring John up to date when he comes in."

"Fine" Toby says. "James, we just completed our first full day of an official investigation, and I've got some exciting news for you. We have discovered that there was possibly a fifth man connected to the robbery who escaped detection because he was probably the getaway driver for the thieves we guessed, and waited outside the store until the others finished the job. We don't know his identity yet, but hopefully some leads that we are developing will eventually lead us to who he is."

Toby then tells James the details of their investigation to this point. Needless to say, James was flabbergasted to say the least, at the rapidity and progress they had made.

"Tell me exactly what you need, to continue on with your work." He tells Toby.

"We need to do some undercover work, which will mean some fake ID's and badges for the men, and fake companies that they supposedly work for." When I meet with you and John, I'll tell you exactly the kind of materials we'll need." James assures him that everything will be provided for them.

"Meet with John and myself the first thing in the morning. We'll call you when we're ready to meet."

"That's great" Toby responds.

After going home that evening, Rod meets his wife Andrea dressed only in a see through negligee, with her body silhouetted in the see through material. Her smooth dark skin was supple and smooth, and her beautiful face and full lips looked extremely inviting. He snuggled up behind her, running his hands over her full dark breasts until her black nipples were visible through the material. His hands roamed inside the negligee and down between her parted thighs. She was wet to his touch, and she could feel his response from behind.

I can't wait until I eat Rod says, as he leads Andrea into the bedroom. They have now been married for over a year, and are expecting their first child. Unlike most couples today, they chose not to know what kind of baby that they would have.

"That takes away from the excitement and mystery" Rod had told Andrea, and she agreed. They talked about how they parents did not know either.

"I guess that makes us odd balls" Andrea had said.

"Odd balls ... So what! Odd balls we are," Rod retorted defiantly.

Their lovemaking was heated, wild, wet and uninhibited, lasting for almost an hour. Rod entered her from behind for fear of damaging her pregnancy, if he made love to her from the front. Afterward they ate a meal of Collard and Kale Greens, Ham Hocks, corn bread and candied sweet potatoes. This made Rod remember one of the reasons why he married her.

Early the next morning, Toby planned to hand out his assignments to each investigator as soon as he hears from quarters. While waiting to hear from the corporate office, they all talk about their feelings of how things are going. Toby tells them what he expects from them in the next phase of the investigation. He wants Rod, Dick and Jeremy to go undercover as **marketing consultants** for the cigar manufacturer, and get as much information about the ten people who had purchased the cigars.

He assigned three of them to each investigator, with Dick getting four.

"Here's what I'm looking for," he tells them" I want as much background and family information that they're willing to share with, things like their siblings, jobs, parents, grandparents, the cars they drive, that kind of stuff. We will run police checks on them from here. Ralph, I want you to follow up later, and gather all the information you can as an undercover **Preventive family health care agent for the state.**"

"I need to get this information to corporate headquarters, so they can get started doing everything that we need them to do." He said as he disappeared through the door leading into the corporate office. While he was gone, the boys continued to discuss the case and its ramifications.

Upon Toby's returned, he informed the group that the office would need at least a couple of days to get everything together. He then addressed Ralph specifically.

"I want information about the family's health concerns, histories of illnesses. Genetic predispositions such as cancer, high blood pressure, diabetes, and things like that."

He then asks the group if anyone had any questions about anything that he covered.

"I feel like they will cooperate more with Dick's line of questioning for preventive health care, than they will with our questions as marketing consultants," Jeremy said.

"That may be the case" Toby admitted, "But that's where you'll have to use your ingenuity and instincts" Toby replied.

"We could tell them that we are trying to compile a profile of the kinds of people that order our product, in order to develop a marketing campaign for TV and advertising purposes" Dick suggested.

"That's the kind of ingenuity that I'm talking about using" Toby beamed. "You guys are going to be just fine. I can feel it."

There were no more comments from the group, and Toby leaned back in his chair, lit up his pipe, and relaxed, feeling very good and comfortable with everything, as he waited to hear from James and John. He questioned them about why there has been no news at all about the missing ruby.

"If the ruby is worth fifty thousand dollars, it must be a sizable chunk that must be cut down, in order to sell without raising a myriad of questions." Dick offered.

"That's a very distinct possibility," Ralph added.

"Are there any diamond cutters in this area that might do that?" Rod asked.

"It might be worth looking into," Toby said. "If anyone would know, it would be Mr. Smith. I'll check with him when we get together next time."

"You told us earlier that you had some misgivings about him," Dick asked, "What were they?"

"Well, when I questioned him about our concerns, he gave me some satisfactory answers, bit I'm still not completely satisfied, but I'll accept them for now."

"Especially now that his insurance company is hesitant to cover the expense to insure it" Jeremy added.

"He may not like all of the extra questioning," Ralph said.

"Then my answer to him was why not. We are leaving no stone unturned." Toby responded.

After the meeting was over, he tells the group that there was nothing else to do until he hears from corporate, and then he would notify each one when they would reconvene. If anyone needed him in the meantime, call him on his cell phone. Toby enjoys the peace and quietness of his office and the pleasure of his pipe as he goes over the events of the day. It was not long before the phone interrupted his solitude. It was a client wanting information about the case that Toby was doing for him.

The next afternoon, Toby gets a call from John and James to meet with them about the investigation. Toby responded immediately. They had the fake ID's, badges, and cell phones for each investigator, along with the vehicles for them to use, complete with plastic names of the businesses the investigators reportedly were from, plastered on the sides for verification purposes.

"What do you think?" James asked.

'This exceeds my expectations." Toby acknowledged.

"This is the fluid nature of our relationship" John said.

There was nothing else to be said, so Toby left to call the guys to come to the office.

Once they were all assembled in the investigation room, Toby lays down the ground rules for the impending investigation.

"All of you have already been given your assignments. Does anyone have further questions about anything?"

No one had any questions.

"When you have completed your assignments, you need to go back to work for the corporation until you hear back from me."

Just then Toby's phone rang. It was a call from a client needing to talk with him. The three investigators leave the office and load up in their vehicles to begin their work. Toby picks up the phone to hear from a very distraught client about a case that he was on. His bosses were right, this will be a very taxing operation, he thought to himself, but he has to be busy to keep his agency solvent.

Jeremy, Rod and Dick, begin each questioning the three names of the persons given to them by Toby, each one posing as marketing agents for the cigar company. They work well into the late hours of the afternoon. After meeting later in the office, they each report their findings to Toby.

"I had no success at all, getting any new information from the three persons that were on my list," reported Jeremy.

"The same here" Rod and Dick each echoed.

"That's OK" Toby tells them "Your work did just what we set out for it to do, and now It's now time to run a police investigation on each one of them. Dick, I want you in charge of this operation."

Dick nods his agreement.

"I'll call each of you when I need you again. In the meantime, I'll have Ralph follow up with his work as the community health care rep. The three detectives expressed their appreciation to Toby for allowing them to do their first undercover work.

"It was truly an experience we will never forget. The fake ID's and vehicles worked like a charm" said Rod.

"I did have a couple of people say how pleased they were to be a part of a marketing plan," Jeremy reported. That certainly showed how effective the work by the corporation was."

After the room cleared, Toby settled down in his chair, lit his pipe, and contemplated his next move. First he called James and John to tell them that he was releasing the three boys back to them for the time being, as well as telling them what a marvelous job they did in furnishing his agency with the materials that they put together for the undercover work.

"I will keep a record of the time they worked for me, and send a copy of their hours, along with the reimbursement to Wingate, when the investigation is through. I'll call you when I need them again." He finished.

"Great! That's exactly how this system is supposed to work," beamed John and echoed by James.

Toby shortly there afterwards, returned the call of the exasperated client who tearfully called him earlier. It was now time for him to get back to work, while Ralph prepared to get underway.

"I'll call you when I need Ralph," Toby tells James on the phone.

Ralph had all ten of the names on the list to investigate, which meant that his work would take a much longer time than the other three. He was searching for personal family information of a delicate and often sensitive nature. His work would begin in a day or two, following the police report of the three investigator's work.

Dick calls Toby a day later.

"We have finished the police report of the persons that Rod, Jeremy and me interviewed. They all came up clean except for a man named Hank Spaulding, Dick tells Toby.

"During his investigation, I'll alert Ralph to keep an eye out for the vehicle described by one of the residents, seen parked near the scene of the crime." Toby finished.

"Sounds like a plan" Dick said.

Every one of Reliford investigators were assembled in the investigation room the next day.

"We received Dick's police report on the person's you visited, and they came up with nothing on each of them, except for a man named Hank Spaulding." Toby told the group.

"At this point that doesn't mean a whole lot," he added.

"He was one of the persons that I talked to," said Jeremy. "Seemed like a nice enough fellow."

Going to the chalkboard, Toby begins a group discussion of the case.

"What kinds of things are you thinking about the case?" Toby wanted to know.

"Why has there been absolutely no word about the stolen ruby?" Jeremy asked.

"Yeah, I was thinking the same thing. You would think that something would have surfaced by now" Rod added.

"Maybe it could be that the diamond has not surfaced, because whoever has it is hesitant about doing anything for one, it's still too soon to do anything," Secondly, because if it's too big to sell in its current size, it may have to be cut smaller in order to sell it in pieces" Dick offered.

"That would be my line of reasoning as well" Toby chimed in. "Good observation, Dick" he said. "What about the rest of you?" he asks the group.

"Now that you've mentioned it that sounds like the most plausible explanation" Jeremy added.

"So where do you think this leaves us?" Toby pressed on.

"Examining everything that we can about each family in order to see if anything surfaces, and any clues to a reason for hiding it, seems like the best approach to continue"

"I agree" Toby said. "And how will this information be gathered?"

"Since all of our people investigated have turned up nothing, it appears that we need to hope that Ralph uncovers some information from his work with the history of the families he investigates, to offer any clues." Dick added.

There was nothing else offered by anyone else present.

"Then, would you say that this report ready to pass on to corporate? Toby asked.

"I would say so, so don't have anything else" Jeremy suggested. The others agreed.

"Then it's settled. I'll tell James and John that we're now ready for Ralph. Agree?"

They all agreed that that should be the next thing that needs to be done. Toby did not want any action to be done without the group's complete approval. This is the way that he wanted the process to work since this is their investigation. He then records the information on the chalk board about their meeting, and the group's decision to call Ralph.

Satisfied, Toby dismisses the group, and enjoys a few moments with his pipe before calling James and John. After making that phone call, he then turns his attention to the case of the distraught client that he was currently working with. He was hopeful that this case would be finished in a matter of a few days, and that he would then be able to send the corporation his first payment of a completed investigation. This excited him a great deal, because it would legitimize his existence as the company's only private investigator. While waiting for Ralph to come, Toby gives his secretary instructions to prepare the time sheets, for each investigator to be turned in to the corporate headquarters at the appropriate time.

When Toby meets with Ralph, he instructs him about what he wants done.

"During the course of your investigation, I want you to keep an eye out for the vehicle that was described by one of the residents that we talked to earlier, who described vaguely the type of car they saw."

Ralph told him that he fully understood what he wanted, and would certainly make it a point to do that.

On his first visit, he meets a girl who mesmerizes him at first sight. It began when he knocked on the door of the first name on his list. The woman who answered the door was one of the most gorgeous creatures he had ever laid his eyes on. She looked to be in her early twenties, with long brunette hair, brown eyes, and a figure to make a priest second guess his celibacy. He was so taken aback by her that he simply gawked.

"May I help you?" She said in a soft angelic voice. Ralph was a confirmed bachelor, and often teased Rod and Jeremy about being married, and no longer able to play the field. But this was a game changer! Ralph was embarrassed for staring when she asked him if there was something wrong.

"No, no. everything's fine," he stammered, pulling out his ID card. "My name is Ralph, and I'm a community health care consultant from the state, doing research on family preventive health care."

"Oh, how interesting," she began, " My name is Karen, and I'm a social work student at the university, and health care issues with families are of primary concern for me, because my family'does not pay enough attention to family genetics or health issues that may be hereditary."

"Wow, I didn't expect this," He said flabbergasted. "That's just the reason what I'm here talk about."

"Oh, how interesting" She responded," Won't you come in?"

Ralph goes inside and is escorted to the sofa in the middle of the room. It was a quaint room, decorated with a woman' touch, he noticed.

"Are your parent's home? He asked.

"No they're at work. I'm here on a fall break from school."

"Which school do you go to?" he asked.

"Wayne State. I'm a junior there" she answered.

"You're kidding" Ralph said "That's my almamater. I graduated from there last year." he told her.

They resumed talking while Ralph continued to be mesmerized by her, and she obviously was very much attracted to him as well He had to really concentrate on what he was there for! It caused him to wonder for the first time, if there really is such a thing as love at first sight.

"You can probably answer the questions that I was going to ask your parents."

"I'll do my best," she responded.

He asked her a series of questions that he had prepared about family illnesses that he used previously with other families, such as what family members died from and when, family genetic predispositions to illnesses such as diabetes, cancer, high blood pressure, etc. She did a good job, he ascertained with her answers.

He was intrigued with her attending Wayne State.

"Do you go to any of the football games at home?" he asked her.

"Yes. I love football and go to as many games as I can, as long as it doesn't interfere with my studies."

"Well, next week we have a home game that I plan to go to. I'd sure love to take you with me, if you want to go" he said.

"That sounds like fun," she responded with a dazzling smile. "I'd love to."

After saying their goodbye's, Ralph left her house very exhilarated and excited. It was all he could think about as he made his way to his next visit. As he drove, something caught his eye as he neared the house he was going to. He caught his breath at what he saw. Parked on the street in front of the house, was a car very much like the one that Toby told him to be on the alert about. Ralph's heart was racing as he parked his car. He got out and walked up to the house, when he heard a lawn mower running in the back yard. He rang the doorbell, but no one answered. His curiosity got the best of him, and he went over to the car and peered inside through an open window. Low and behold, there in the ashtray of the car, he saw cigar butts, just like the one's the security guard at the jewelry gave them! He could hardly contain his excitement as his heart felt as though it was going to burst from his chest.

He reached inside and retrieved two butts from the ashtray, and immediately took them back to the office to do an analysis with the DNA he already had. They were a perfect match! Ralph literally ran to Toby's desk bursting with excitement.

"Whoa," Toby said. "Slow down, Ralph. I've never seen you like this before" he stated even before laying down his pipe.

"I did it! I did it!" he repeated, "We've found the missing person he spouted, putting the butts down on Toby's desk.

"Slow down and tell me what you're talking about, Ralph," Toby said wide eyed at Ralph's excitement.

"I found the car that you told me to look out for, and these cigar butts were in the ashtray in it. It was the same man that the police told us about having a criminal record."

"That would be Hank Spaulding"

"Yes, he's the one."

"Did you get a chance to talk with him?" Toby asked.

"No he was in his back yard cutting grass."

"Then he doesn't know that you have this information." Toby said.

"No," Ralph replied.

"Good. That gives us advantage. We have enough evidence to link him with the others. Even though what we have is only circumstantial, it's enough to have him picked up and arrested on suspicion. Let me call Bob at Headquarters and give him this information, and then invite him join us at our next meeting to begin a plan to arrest Spaulding as a possible accomplice." Toby advises.

"Great idea" Ralph agreed.

"Before we go any further though Ralph, I want you to go back to Spaulding and get all of the information that you can about his family, before we have him picked up," Toby directs him.

"I'll do exactly that," Ralph assures him.

"You couldn't have given me better news," Toby told him. "I'll get the rest of the crew together after I talk with Bob," he says as he picks up his pipe with trembling hands.

He calls the corporate office and tells James and John of the latest developments, after he had talked with Bob. There was as much excitement with all of them as it was with him and Ralph.

"It seems as though we are making significant strides, especially with Bob's reaction that you just told us about," James said.

Toby gets all of his crew together that afternoon to go over plans for the upcoming with Bob. When everyone was present in the investigation room, Toby goes to the chalk board, and writes down this latest bit of information.

"Where do you think this leaves us?" Toby asked the team.

"This Spaulding fellow, could he possibly be the getaway driver for the robbers?" Rod asked the group.

"Well, that's not a certainty, but it's highly probable that he could be." Dick added." All we have at this point is just circumstantial evidence, which is much better than none at all though."

"What else could it be," muttered Jeremy. "After all, he was sitting in the alley at or near the time of the heist."

"That has not been proven yet," Dick warned. "All that we know for sure is that a car was spotted in the alley at or near the time of the robbery by a witness, but Spaulding was not identified as the one sitting in it. Just because he has a past criminal record does not mean that he's guilty of anything" Rod said.

"That's true" Ralph said, "But it does make him our number one suspect, and also means that he may be connected with the other perps."

"Do the rest of you agree that we now have a number one suspect in the case?" Toby queried.

Every one of his investigators nodded their heads in agreement, and Toby writes this down on his board.

"If he is connected to the other gang members as their driver, is there any way of knowing that he has any knowledge of the ruby?" Rod asked.

"First of all, we're getting way ahead of ourselves, and are now talking about two separate issues." Dick warned.

"I agree wholeheartedly with Dick at this point. Let's not let our imaginations run away with things here." Toby says.

Everyone present agreed that there was nothing to hang their hats on.

With that, Toby writes that down on the board, along with the DNA results of Ralph's work, and the police report of Spaulding's police record.

"Let's examine where we are at this point. First of all, we have no real evidence of anything to pin on anyone. But we do have a primary suspect that some tangible evidence points to as a culprit. "What else are you all thinking about the case?" Toby wanted to know.

"It's about the diamond. The deeper we go with this investigation, the more questions come up about this missing diamond that amazes me," Jeremy says.

"Things like what?" Dick asks him.

"Why is it that the diamond is still missing, and nothing is ever heard about it, while everyone seems to have such a vested interest in it?" Rod stated.

"First of all, the thieves seem to want it very badly, and it is the only thing not recovered to this point. If they know anything, they are not willing to talk about it. Also, the store owner seems to want it so badly, that he's willing to absorb a loss in order to retrieve it," Toby added.

"One thing I do know," contributed Dick "When you add all of this together, no one or nothing is to be excluded as a suspect."

"You're right, Dick, and this includes the store owner as well, and the person or persons that he purchased the ruby from. It's possible that the person who sold it to him could be the thief." Toby added.

"Sounds like a plan to me," Rod said.

"I think it's about time that we plan to have Spaulding picked up as a suspect. I'll call Bob and arrange a meeting with him tomorrow."

"What will he be charged with seeing that we have no evidence to charge him with," Rod asked.

"If nothing else, suspicion, conspiracy or vagrancy," Dick suggested. "We won't be able to hold him except for questioning, even if he falls for the trap we plan to set."

At the meeting the next day, a plan was put in place to lay a trap for Spaulding with the police department and his office. The plan was laid in great detail. He instructed Ralph to pay Spaulding a visit and also tell him about the upcoming police investigation.

"Well, unless anyone has anything more to add, I think that this should bring an ending to this meeting." Toby concluded. There were no further comments, so things came to an end. Everyone but Ralph was dismissed.

"Well Ralph, it's up to you now to plant the seed for Spaulding to bite,"

"He'll bite like a catfish" Ralph said.

Toby called James and John to give them an update on the case, and settled in for a relaxing time with his pipe, and to call Peg. He was a little apprehensive, but hopeful at the same time that Ralph would uncover something on Spaulding to move the investigation forward. At his point, there was absolutely no place else to go. He now became painfully aware of the feeling of futility in this case that the police must have been experiencing.

In the meantime, Ralph went back to Spaulding's house as he was directed to do so by Toby, to continue his undercover work as a community health rep. He knocked on the front door and a short, burly man in his fifties, with a two week old beard that needed trimming, and unkempt hair answered.

"Mr. Spaulding?" asked Ralph.

"That's me, and who are you?" he asked Ralph in a gruff voice. Ralph pulled out his ID, and showed it to him.

"I'm here to ask you some questions about your family's health, as part of our emphasis on a preventive health care survey."

"OK, I don't have much time, but come on in," he told Ralph.

Once inside, Ralph took a seat in a chair in the living room. As he looked around, the room was unkempt, just like you would expect from a man living alone.

"Do you have any brothers and sisters," he asked.

"Yeah, I have one brother and sister," Spaulding answered.

"And are you the oldest?"

"No, I'm in the middle."

"Are your parents still living?"

"My mother is. She's living with my sister.my father died years ago from cancer."

"So cancer runs in your family?"

"Yes, that and high blood pressure."

"What about your brother and sister. Are they healthy?"

"Yeah, they're OK"

"Do they live nearby?"

"My brother lives in Iowa, but my sister is here."

"Could I have her address to talk with her as well?" Ralph asked him.

"Yeah, I don't care," he answered Ralph, giving him her address. "My mother is living with her, because she's sick."

"Well, I don't have anything more," Ralph tells him. "I certainly appreciate your help and cooperation."

"That's OK" he was told.

"Oh, by the way," Ralph said before leaving," The police have got a lead about the robbery, by someone who saw a man sitting in the alley in a car behind the jewelry store, smoking, close to the time of the robbery, and they plan to investigate that area thoroughly.' He added before leaving.

"He noticed the shocked look on the man's face before he left. He was certain that the man clearly got the message. He left Spaulding's house with a good feeling, and a great sense of satisfaction at the results he got. He was a little surprised, however, at the ease of his visit, which he thought might have been a little more apprehensive and tension filled.

Before heading back to the office, he stopped by to see Karen. She was constantly on his mind, and was very excited to see him when he stopped by. He couldn't believe his luck with her, but could not help but wonder how many other guys had a keen interest in her. She told him that she was too busy with her school work to pay much attention to boys, and that her mother wanted it to be that way anyway. He liked her mother already.

Many times when you want something very much in life, something negative often seems to crop up and interferes with it. Being pursued by a host of other men, who also found her extremely beautiful, was the primary reason for Ralph being a little apprehensive about his luck with her. But thanks in part for the mother's role in this case his uneasiness was soon being dispelled. Maybe these were the same kind of thoughts that Rod and Jeremey had about Andrea and Beth, before they married them, he wondered.

After leaving her house, he met with Toby in the office, and told him that he had gotten all of the information he could about Spaulding's family.

'Ralph, you did you remember to tell him about the police department planning to follow up on a tip from an informant, that a man was seen sitting in a car outside of the jewelry store, smoking during the robbery, and that we are planning to investigate the sight for any evidence we can find, especially cigarette butts, or any other items that he may have discarded. That's the seed we want to plant in his mind?" Toby queried.

"I told him everything that you wanted me to tell him" Ralph responded.

"I should have known," Toby said a little ashamed for doubting Ralph's credibility, and told him so.

"Thanks OK" Ralph replied. "After all, you're the boss."

The plan to set the trap for Spaulding was for everyone to wait in the darkness in the security officer's room, and wait for Spaulding to return to look for anything he feared might he left behind."

"This is based on the theory that criminals always return to the scene of the crime." He said.

Now that the plan has been laid, it was now time to wait until that night to spring the trap. The police, Bob, Toby, and his investigators, would all meet that night in the security guard's room to wait for Spaulding to take the bait. They would all arrive in unmarked cars, and park on the street nearby.

Meanwhile, Jeremy and Beth were enjoying a quiet moment together waiting for Toby to call, with Jeremy feeling very sexually aroused, as he watched Beth in the kitchen getting dinner ready, wearing only an apron and a top that barely covered her large breasts that bounced around with every movement.

They were now married for a little over a year, and had been talking about having a baby.

"Are you trying to send me a message that you're ready to start making a baby?" he asked her jokingly.

"I don't know what you're talking about" Beth answered coyly.

"You know full well what I'm talking about" he said, coming up behind her and putting his arms around her, and cupping both of her breasts in his hand.

"You know how I can tell when you feel this way?"

"No I don't, you tell me."

"When you get horny, your nipples get big and hard like they are now," he said gently caressing them with his finger and thumb. Beth moaned audibly and leaned back against him, rubbing her butt against the massive bulge that she could feel growing in his pants, and pressing against her.

"This moment reminds me so clearly of last year, during the trial of you and Jeremy back home, when you took me to the park for the first time, and we wanted each other so badly, but held off at the last minute because we didn't want our first time to be in the back seat of a car. Do you remember that?" Beth moaned with a husky voice full of lust, as she placed here hands on top of Jeremy's and moved them over her taught nipples.

"Uh, huh," Jeremy was able to breathe. "That was then, but this now," he whispered, picking her up in his arms, carrying her into the bedroom.

"I'm going to finish now what I started then," he said laying her down on her back, and slowly removing the thin top, and as he spread her legs. She was not wearing any panties, which was another clue to Jeremy that she was more than ready. When he put his hand between her legs, she was sopping wet, and gasped loudly. When he removed his pants, he was hard as a rock and had a massive erection that had to be satisfied. Beth was more than willing to oblige him, spreading her legs as wide as she could to accept him deep into her.

Shortly after they were through with their lovemaking, the phone rang, it was Toby.

"Jeremy, you need to come to the office right away with the other guys, we have to get ready for tonight."

"I'm on my way" Jeremy replied with excitement.

That night as darkness fell the security guard's tiny office was full of people. The air was filled with excitement and anticipation. This was a first for Toby's investigators and it showed. They whispered excitedly to each other, in stark difference to the police and Toby, who just waited patiently, with their eyes glued to window.

"What will he be charge with?" a voice was heard to say in the darkness.

"Suspicion of robbery" the familiar voice of Bob was heard "We do have him suspected of being connected with the ones in custody, so that justifies our actions here."

"Let's hope we're right and he takes the bait," Toby was heard to say.

"Even if he doesn't, we still have enough evidence to pick him up at his house, and take him in for questioning" Bob reiterated.

Just then, the headlights of a car peered through the blackness of the night, and shone in the alley.

"That would Spaulding" Bob said, as a scurry of rustling clothes and equipment could be heard in the room. A dark figure was seen emerging from the car that came to a halt in the alley. As the figure moved about carrying a flashlight shining on the ground, it was obvious that someone was searching for something.

"This is the moment we've waited for," Bob said, "Let's take him."

The door was flung open, and immediately the yard was full of the men with flashlights, spilling out of the office, shining a flood of light on a startled and unaware victim who covered his eyes from the piercing glare of light blinding his vision. It was Spaulding alright!

"Spaulding, you're under arrest," barked Bob, as his men moved in quickly to pin his arms behind his back.

"What is this all about," shrieked a startled Spaulding.

After reading him his rights, Bob told him that he was under arrest for the robbery of the jewelry store the other day.

"Robbery? What are you talking about.? I don't know anything about no robbery."

"Drop try to play innocent Spaulding. We've got you dead to rights. You drove the getaway car for the thieves who robbed the jewelry store. We've got the evidence on you."

"What evidence and what getaway car are you talking about?" a bewildered Spaulding asked."

"The car we're talking about was spotted by one of the residents nearby, while you sat in the alley during the robbery.

"I don't know anything about no robbery" a stubborn Spaulding responded.

"Drop the act Spaulding," barked Bob. "You know very well what we're talking about."

"What are you talking about?" challenged Spaulding.

"The cigar butts that you threw on the ground while you waited on your buddies to finish their work inside the store.

"What buddies are you talking about and what about the cigar butts?"

"We found the same butts in the ashtray of your car while you were cutting your yard in the back of your house."

"So what, that doesn't prove a thing, plenty people smoke cigars. I have stopped in that alley many times to take a break from people, and to get away for a while, but not at the time you're talking about."

"Very few smoke the kind you smoke, and sit in a vacant alley smoking them when a crime is being committed.'

"Tell that to the police at headquarters. By the way, you know that all of the thieves have been caught and the stolen contraband has been recovered. I bet they will be glad to see you." Bob said wryly.

"I don't know anything about thieves or contraband."

"Well, well, we'll see when you get to headquarters," Bob replied.

Bob then instructs his officers to put the victim in one of the unmarked squad cars, and take him to the station for booking and fingerprinting. After they had left, he turned his attention to Toby, his investigators, and thanking the security officer for the use of his office and his help.

"Now that all of the thieves are in custody, and the stolen items are all recovered, except for the missing ruby, if it exists at all, our work has come to a halt in this case, and the rest of it now remains in your hands. All we have to do now is get the goods on Spaulding somehow." I'll let you know how the interrogation of him goes tonight." Bob finished.

After the room clears, Toby told his crew that he would see them in the morning at the office to discuss their next agenda.

"Other than having all of the perps in custody, we're right back where we started from to begin with," Rod noted, as they began their meeting.

"That's true to a certain extent," Toby responded, "But don't forget, if it were not for your work in this investigation, the police would not have found the other suspect that was not in the photo, or connected to the crime."

"That's true," Dick added. "The police are certainly much further ahead now in this case than we were before."

'I don't see anything else we can do at this point," Toby said, "Except have Ralph follow up on his work with Spaulding's family. Does anyone else have any suggestions or comments?"

"We're at a stalemate concerning the missing ruby," Jeremy added. "I can't help but wonder if Spaulding really has no knowledge of the ruby."

Later on that night at police headquarters, Spaulding was placed in the interrogation room for questioning.

"I'm not answering any questions without an attorney present," Spaulding shouted belligerently.

After reading him his rights, an attorney was called in for Spaulding.

"OK, let's try this again, Bob said. What were you doing sitting In the alley, in a car during the robbery? We have a witness who saw you."

"It wasn't me they saw."

"Where were you during the time in question?"

"I was at home watching television."

"Can you prove that?"

"Can you prove I wasn.t? I live alone"

"The cigar butts that the security guard found in the alley the next day following the robbery, matched the ones found in the ashtray of your car"

"How long had these butts been in the alley?"

"The guard said that he had not seen them before until after the robbery."

"That's probably because he had not looked before, because he had no reason to. Like I said before, I've sat in that alley on several occasions."

"Why did you come back in the alley with a flashlight shining on the ground, if it wasn't because you were looking for something that you thought was left behind?"

"I was only there out of curiosity about what a health care investigator mentioned, when he talked to me about a break that the police had from a witness near the jewelry store, about something left the alley following the robbery."

"What do you know about a missing ruby that has not been found yet following the robbery?"

"For the tenth time, I don't know anything about a robbery, or a missing ruby."

"Would you agree to take a lie detector test to prove that?"

"For what, I don't even know what you're talking about, and I'm not taking a lie detector test to prove nothing."

"We'd be interested to know how your buddies will react when they see you in the line up tomorrow." Bob finished.

"What buddies are you talking about?"

"You'll see in the morning. Take him to his cell," Bob directed his officers.

The next morning, the thieves were assembled in a hidden room to view the lineup which included Spaulding along with three other persons. When the Lineup was over, Spaulding was taken into the room with the other prisoners. There were looks of surprise on their faces, but no one said anything.

"Any of you know this man?" Bob asked them.

They did nothing except shake their heads. He asked them a second time, but just got the same reaction. After everything was finished, Bob informed his officers that he would have to release Spaulding.

"I have no reason to hold him without any evidence, and no identification of him from any of the Prisoners in custody. I was hoping that they would finger him, but I guess that code of not snitching on one another that criminals often have, is the reason."

Bob tells Spaulding later, that because he is a prime suspect in this case, that he was not to leave town or travel anywhere without first notifying the police.

"Don't worry, I'm not going anywhere because of my mother's condition. I told you that you were just wasting your time" He said with a smirk.

"Bob called me last night at home, and told me that Spaulding refused to take a lie detector test about the ruby, saying that his testimony was the same as his buddies.

"Well, you certainly can't make anyone take it against their will," Dick added.

"It is really, strange how no one knows anything about this ruby," Toby said. "I need to examine Mr. Smith's inventory of the stolen jewelry. I know the police have already done that, but I want to see it for myself."

"I can see why his insurance company is having their problem with the diamond, just as we are," Jeremy added.

Everyone in the room just sat with their chins in their hands, and blank looks staring into space as their collective minds raced in silence. It seemed like an eternity, but it was only for a minute or two.

"Well, I need to get busy notifying the corporation of where we are, and release all of you back to them, so you can go back to your jobs. If Ralph gets any new news to report after his investigation with Spaulding's family, I'll notify each one of you. In the meantime, I'm going to clear our chalk board because we have nothing to add to it."

No one had anything to say, so the meeting was adjourned, and the investigation room emptied out. Toby took time to relax in his office, and light up his pipe filling the room with its aromatic aroma, before calling James and John. He updated them of the latest developments.

"Bob called us this morning, and gave us the details about the arrest, the interrogation, and finally the release of the primary suspect due to a lack of evidence.'" John said.

"That sounds much worse than it really is," replied James "But much better than where we were before. At least we know who the missing guy is, and it's only a matter of time before we nab him."

Toby smiled broadly, and drew deeply on his pipe, leaning back and relaxing in his chair.

"I have sent my crew back to you for the time being, with instructions to recall them if needed. "I will bill Mr. Smith for services rendered to this point, and send you the proceeds. Until something else comes up, I'm going to continue to follow up with my own private investigations." Toby concluded.

"Great! This is going better than expected," James chimed in. "Stay in touch, and keep up with the good work."

"Will do," Toby assured them

Meanwhile, Ralph was on the trail of visiting Spaulding's family. When he arrived at his sister's house who caring for their sick mother, he rang the front door bell. An attractive middle aged brunette with a good figure answered the door.

Ms. Roberts?" Ralph inquired not knowing if she was widowed or divorced, seeing no ring on her hand.

"Yes, and who are you?" she answered politely.

"I'm Ralph Simon," he introduced himself, handing her his business card and displaying his ID badge.

"Come in," she invited him, opening the door wider. She invited him to sit on the couch and make himself comfortable.

"Can I get you something to drink, coffee, tea, or something cold?"

"Oh, coffee would be fine"

She left and Ralph surveyed the room. She was an immaculate house keeper. He was amazed at how different she was from her brother. He wondered if they really had the same mother. When she returned, Ralph thanked her for her hospitality, and proceeded to question her with the same line of questioning used in all of his former inquiries.

"Your brother informed me that you are caring for his sick mother."

"Yes, I'm afraid she's dying, and doesn't have much longer," She said tearfully.

"I'm so sorry to hear that," Ralph said sympathetically. "What is she dying from?"

"Cancer in It's in the last stages."

"Can I meet her?" Ralph asked.

"I'll see if she wants to," She responded. "By the way, Ralph, call me Brenda."

"I will from now on," Ralph said. She was so easy to talk to, and had a wonderful personality and warm smile. Upon her return, he was pleased to hear that she said it was OK.

"I wouldn't take any longer than five minutes or so." Brenda told him. "You'll see how weak she is when you go in. She prefers to be called Gladys"

Ralph assured her that he would only stay a few minutes. The more he looked at her, the more she was growing on hm. She was very attractive, not a beauty per say, but for her age which he guessed to be about in her early fifties, she was really nice looking, with shapely legs he noticed. If he were twenty years older ... his thoughts were interrupted when he entered the room. He was immediately conscious of her deteriorated appearance and weakened condition. It was obvious that she didn't have much time left. Brenda sat wiping her eyes.

"Momma, this is the young man that I told you about."

"My, but you are a nice looking fellow," she managed to say weakly.

"Why thank you Gladys. You certainly have a lovely daughter, and she's very nice. You did a marvelous job with her."

"Why that's a very thoughtful thing to say. I did my best. Brenda told me who you were, and that you've met my son."

"Yes I did." Ralph replied.

The two talked for a few minute more as Brenda sat quietly.

"If there's anything I can do, have Brenda call me."

"Just keep me in your prayers."

"I will," Ralph promised.

After he and Brenda left the room, Ralph gave Brenda another one of his cards, and wrote his cell phone number on the backside of it.

"I want you to have my personal number to call me with any news about your mother's condition, and if you have anything that you would like to discuss with me, please call."

She promised him that she would as he left. He left with a heavy heart for her and her mother. They both were so nice. He drove back to the office where he met with Toby.

"Nothing new to report "he says to Toby "Just another routine visit."

"I wouldn't classify it as just routine. You never know what it might produce down the road." He advised. "I think you need to go back to work now. Good job, Ralph. The others have already gone back. Stay in touch."

Toby was satisfied now, that there was absolutely nothing else for them to do. He had gone over Mr. Smith's inventory himself, and found nothing new that the police hadn't. He billed Mr. Smith for the service of his agency up to this point, and turned the proceeds over to the corporate headquarters. He wished that he could think of nothing else to try as he puffed on his pipe. At this point they could only hope and wait for something to happen. They were at a stalemate for sure.

The fall air was brisk, with a mild breeze, as Ralph and Karen, hand in hand, made their way over the campus grounds headed for the stadium, to see the huge homecoming game between their own Wayne State and Pinehurst State. Both of them were dressed warmly in winter coats and gloves. Ralph wore a fitted cap covering his ears, while Karen wore a big furry hat that covered everything but her eyes.

This was the favorite time of the year for both of them. The leaves on the trees had turned a beautiful burnt orange, and some were partially red. As they tread over the brown grass covered with fallen leaves that crunched under their feet, they were very happy and felt very much alive together.

Ralph could not take his eyes off of her, as much of her as he could see, and she constantly squeezed his hand as they walked. He had never been as enamored with a woman before as he was with Karen.

"I need to confess," he tells her. "You make me very happy, and I feel so close to you already. You've never been a stranger, Karen, it's like I've known you all of my life."

"I know," she answered him, "Isn't it strange that two strangers can meet, and never feel like they're strangers at all. When I first saw you, you captivated me so completely."

"Same here," Ralph confessed. "You were all that I could think about. It makes this so called confirmed bachelor wonder whether or not there is such a thing as love at first sight. My friend Rod told me over a year ago, that before he and Andrea were married, that he knew that she was always going to be the only girl in his life from that moment on, and she swore it was like that for her as well. I also told him that all of that didn't make sense to me."

"I don't know about love at first sight, because no one really understands love, which means that it will always be a mystery as it should be. All I know is that I cannot explain why I feel the way I do at this moment." She said as she pressed closer to him and snuggled her head on his shoulder. He wrapped her completely in his arms while gazing into her eyes.

"The only way that I can tell anything about what's going on right now, is that it must begin as a magnetic attraction between two people when they meet. It just happens with no explanation or reason. You can't control feelings, only what you do with them. They just come." He said.

They're a lot like dreams. No one knows where they come from either most of the time, and hardly ever make any sense." She added.

"Have you ever met two complete strangers, and feel closer to one than to the other? Neither has done anything to you or for you, yet you feel drawn to one and distant to the other." Jeremy asked her.

"Yes, many times."

"It's just unexplainable chemistry is all I can think of, just like now."

They both smiled at each other and continued to walk hand in hand to the stadium. The stadium was packed to the rafters; standing room only. They heard the buzz a mile away. While they were making their way to their seats, Ralph heard Rod and Jeremy call out too him. They made his way over to them as they stood in the center aisle.

"Hey, I know them," exclaimed Karen, as they all shook hands." Rod was an awesome running back a couple of years ago, when I was just a freshman." She continued.

The three of them grinned at each other.

"Rod, and Jeremy, this is Karen," Ralph said introducing them. The two of them shook Karen's hand.

"So Ralph, how did you get this lucky?" Rod said giving Karen an admiring look.

"The same the way that you did with Andrea" Rod replied.

"Do you mean Andrea Bivens?" Karen asked.

"Yes, she's the one. We've been married over a year now, and she's expecting."

"I know her very well. So you're the hunk that she was always talking about."

Rod smiled, blushing.

"You're blushing," Jeremy observed.

"Now how can you tell when a black person blushes?" Rod challenged him.

"I can see it in your eyes, and by your expression and body language."

"You were an awesome Running Back I'm surprise that you didn't go pro." Karen told him.

"I thought about but decided to get married, especially when I was not invited to the combine."

"Look, we can't stand here in the aisle blocking traffic. Let's meet at Joe's Pizza House after the game." Ralph advised.

"Sounds like a plan," responded Rod.

Karen and Ralph found their seats, and had to make their way over several people.

"Man, this place is packed," Ralph said. "Let me go get you something to much on before the game starts,"

"OK, I'll have a hot dog and a soda," Karen told him.

Ralph made it back to his seat just in time for the kickoff. He sat for several minutes, just watching Karen eat.

"I even love the way you chew," he told her.

She nudged him playfully, smiling. Ralph knew at that moment that he would never feel this way again about another woman.

The roar of the crowd was deafening when the kickoff was made. Ralph estimated the crowd to be around fifty thousand. He didn't see an empty seat in the stadium. Ralph put his arm around Karen's shoulder and pulled her close to him. She put her head on his shoulder, and they watched the game like that. The action itself was Nip and Tuck the entire game.

"I thought that the team you play at homecoming was supposed to be a team that you were supposed to beat easily" he said to Karen. Wayne State finally won the game on a last minute field goal to escape going to an overtime period.

The homecoming festivities were very entertaining, and of course, Karen knew both the homecoming king and queen.

After the game, they met Rod and Jeremy in the pizza parlor. They ordered a large pizza and a salad. Karen wanted to know when Rod and Andrea goy married. She really thought a lot of Andrea.

"A year and a half ago" Rod responded" Midway during my senior year. That was just before we got into trouble in Midway down south."

"OH, Yes, I know all about that. That was all that everyone on campus talked about. Your fathers went down there while you were on trial. When both of you returned, you were instant celebrities. And your fathers were heroes."

"I was shocked at the reception we got when we returned to the campus. We didn't know that the student body knew anything about what happened.

"Oh yes! Your fathers had everything put in the newspapers and on television. Everyone at school cheered when they found out the two of you were cleared." Karen said.

"And that is the why all of us are together right now, Me, Rod, Jeremy and Mike. We all work for The Reliford private investigation agency as a result. Their fathers formed the company over a year ago, and hired the sheriff, Toby Reliford from Midway to run it." Ralph explained.

"Do you mean Mike Wingate who works in the police department?"

:Yep, he's the one," Ralph replied. "We are working in conjunction with them on the recent jewelry robbery.

"We had just finished working on an undercover assignment with him." Rod told her.

'An undercover assignment?" asked Karen wide eyed.

"That's the reason I was able to meet you, working undercover as a community health care consultant for the state." Ralph said.

"Wow! I had no clue whatsoever," Karen confessed. Your credentials were so authentic looking. So how are things going?"

"The police have recovered all of the stolen items as you know. They've recovered everything except a thirty thousand dollar ruby that no one seems to know anything about it. And until it's found, they can't close the case. That's the reason that the jewelry store hired our agency to find it, and why Dick is working with us." Jeremy explained.

"Neither the police or us can go any further in the investigation, without a new clue or some kind of information to go on." Rod added.

"Until that happens, when I'm not working at the corporation's chemical company, I can spend as much time as I can with you," Ralph tells Karen.

"Ralph is that you talking?" Rod said in mock surprise. "The same guy that said that I was nuts when I told you that I fell in love with Andrea as soon as we met?"

"And the same guy who said that he will always be a guy that would not get hooked on any female? Ralph, you're not sounding like the same guy!"

"Come on fellas, give me a break here," he pleaded.

Karen just watched the interplay among these friends and only smiled. She was a little embarrassed, but a little flattered at the same time. She put her arm in Ralph's arm with a dazzling smile.

"That's OK, honey, let them talk" she cooed.

They all enjoyed a good laugh together.

Three weeks go by without any significant changes. Toby stayed busy with his private investigations, the boys stayed busy with their jobs in the corporation, and James and John continuing to run Wingate. Toby continues to wrack his brain trying to figure out what it is he's missing or not doing. Mr. Smith is growing more and more aggravated with his insurance company that refuses to budge from their original position.

CHAPTER FOUR

E ARLY IN THE MORNING WHILE Ralph was enjoying a morning cup of coffee, his phone rang. It was Brenda. "Ralph, is that you?" she asked.

"Yes, this is Ralph."

"Ralph, this is Brenda. You told me to call you if I get anything important about my mother's illness. Remember?"

"OH, yes I remember, of course. How are the two **you** doing?"

"I'm doing OK. Mom is failing fast, however. I'm afraid she's about ready for Hospice care. I just discovered something that troubles me, and I just thought that you ought to know about it."

"That's fine. What is it?"

"Mom is close to death now, and she showed me a ruby that my brother Hank gave her. She always wanted an expensive piece of jewelry. But this ruby was so big and expensive looking, that it troubles me."

"I'm glad that you called me on my cell phone instead of the phone on my card, because that was not really my true identity. I was working undercover at the time I met you as a follow up on your brother. I'm really am a private investigator for Reliford Investigations, doing work for Monsero's jewelry store to try and recover the missing ruby. I'm sorry that I had to meet you under false pretense."

That's fine. You were only doing your job."

"I'm glad that you understand"

"I thought that all of the jewels were recovered, and the thieves apprehended and locked up"

"That part is true, everything was found except a big expensive ruby that is still missing. Since your brother is now our primary suspect, you can see how important your call is to me."

"Well, I'm glad that I called you, because I've always had my doubts about him ever since his imprisonment."

"I have a strong hunch that the ruby your mother, has given to her by your brother, is the one that was stolen and missing."

"I have a strong feeling that you might be right. I love my brother, but I've never really trusted him, and have never liked him very much .He can be very Mean."

"I hate to tell you this, but that's the news that I've been waiting to hear. "Your brother has been booked for suspicion of robbery, as part of the gang who robbed of the jewelry store, but we couldn't hold him because we don't have any evidence on him."

"What makes you so certain that he was involved?"

"He was spotted by a person sitting in the alley behind the store when it was robbed. Since he was not in the store at the time of the robbery, he was not identified on the store's video cameras. We found a certain brand of cigar butts in the alley that the person waiting outside was smoking, and we found the same butts in your brother's car."

"Then you sound pretty certain that the person you're looking for is my brother."

"Yes," he responded seeing the look of dejection and hurt on her face. Even in spite of everything, blood is still thicker than water.

"I'm sorry," Ralph offered.

"Thanks. But it's OK."

"I want to see the ruby for myself, and also to bring a gemologist with me to do an appraisal of it if that's OK with you."

"That's fine. Just tell me when.

"As soon as I clear this with my boss, I'll call you back.

"What is it that you want me to do now," she asked.

"I believe that your brother, Hank, will come and get the diamond after you mother has passed, and intends to have it cut to size and sell it."

"And you want me to call you when he picks it up,"

"That's exactly what I need you to do. We need to catch him with the ruby in his possession."

"Normally, hospice will tell us when the time has come to notify all family members to come home when the end is near. That's the time when we are to notify our physician to establish the time of death." Brenda stated.

"That's correct. "Now, this is very, very, important, Brenda. When that time comes, I need for you to call me as soon as possible, so that we can apprehend your brother at his house, with the ruby in his possession."

"Do you have any questions at All for me? Ralph asks her. She said no.

After saying goodbye, Ralph immediately calls Toby.

"Toby, this is Ralph," he said when he heard Toby's voice.

"We've got the break that we need about the missing ruby." Ralph gushed unable to control his excitement. Toby's heart leaped, and his pipe fell out of his hand onto his desk.

"Ralph, slow down and tell me exactly what you're talking about."

Ralph pause long enough to catch his breath and regain control of his emotions. There was an extended pause.

"Well in my follow up on Spaulding's family, I discovered that he has given her a large expensive ruby."

"How did you get this information?"

"His sister Brenda told me"

"What's your next move?" Toby asked.

"She has given me permission to come and see the ruby, and to also bring a gemologist with me to do an appraisal of it."

"Good grief, this is amazing," Toby exclaimed picking up his pipe from his desk. "This is exactly what we've been waiting for!"

Ralph had never heard Toby so excited like this. Normally, he was rather stoic and reserved, seemingly in control all of the time. Ralph felt a rush of excitement because it was him that caused this reaction in his boss. He felt a great sense of pride and satisfaction, because he realized the ramification of this news to the investigation.

Now it was Ralph's turn to ask Toby what his next step would be.

"I'm guessing that Spaulding is planning to get the ruby back after his mother dies, and have it cut down to size, so that he can sell it without suspicion. That appears to be his motive."

"I agree," Ralph replied. l

"Don't mention this to anyone yet," he cautioned Ralph. "I won't say a word to anyone either, even to Mr. Smith, until you've had had a chance to complete your work and get back to me."

"Right," Ralph replied.

After their conversation was through, Toby sat back in his chair, relit his pipe, and puffed on it leisurely, as he replayed the information he had just received from Ralph. This was huge! He couldn't wait to get the report about the ruby, so that they could plan to lay another trap for Spaulding and catch him with the ruby in his possession. Then they would have the evidence they needed to close out the case. He would not say anything even to Bob, until every jot and tittle of this case was over.

After he calmed himself down and relaxed even further, he decided to call Bob and bring him up to date on everything.

"Bob, this is Toby, I've got some exciting news for you."

"It must be good. You certainly sound pumped."

"it appears that we are closing in on the search for the missing ruby. Ralph has found out where the ruby is from Spaulding's sister.

"Where is it?" Bob asked, his voice trembling with excitement.

"It's at her house where her mother is dying from cancer. Spaulding gave it to her soon after the robbery. She's in the final stages, and Hospice will be called in soon. We suspect that after she passes, Hank, her brother will come in and pick the ruby up."

"Did Ralph follow up on my suggestion that he contact Mr. Robinson, the gemologist?"

"Yes. He did exactly as you asked.

"Great. I can't wait until I hget his report, because that will go a long way in determining which direction we'll take. This calls for immediate action on our part here"

"What's your plan?" asked Toby.

"I think that because we're getting so close, I need to begin getting a search warrant for Spaulding's house, so that we can catch him with the goods on him."

"What's the best way to do that?" asked Toby.

"Well, for starters, we'll wait until Ralph calls us when Hospice is notified by Spaulding's sister, and then we'll set up surveillance around his house and wait until he comes home. In the meantime, I'll also get a warrant for his arrest."

Toby and Peg were both elated at the news and celebrated together over several glasses of wine, until both of them were very tipsy. Peg was overwhelmed with joy for Toby and his crew. She watched as his frustration grew over the lack of progress they were not making over the last month or so.

"I'm going to reward you," she told him, standing up and stripping off her top, exposing her full, voluptuous breast s before his feasting eyes. They were still round and shapely even at her age. She reached down and pulled up her nighty, removing her panties and revealing her large pubic area with a wisp of pubic hairs, barely covering her crotch. Toby whisked her up in his arms, and carried her into the bedroom where they make, wild and noisy sex together.

Ralph contacted a known gemologist, referred to him by Bob at police headquarters. He was supposed to be the leading expert in the area when it comes to jewelry and expensive Gems.

"Mr. Robinson," Ralph said introducing himself to a neatly dressed older gentleman with snowy white hair, and friendly smile, "The lieutenant down at police headquarters suggested that I contact you, and ask if you would be willing to go with me and analyze a missing ruby for him when we find it."

"Oh, you must mean Bob and the ruby that was stolen."

"Yes, he spoke very highly of you."

"That's nice to hear. I've worked for Bob before." Mr. Robinson acknowledged.

"I work as an investigator for Reliford investigations, and the police department is working with us to recover the missing ruby."

"When do you need me"

"We don't know right now because the ruby is still missing, but we are making good progress on finding it."

"I'll be here whenever you need me. Tell Bob I wish him well in his investigation."

"I will, and I really appreciate your cooperation, and willingness to help us." Ralph replied as he shook the man's hand and said goodbye. Everything was now set for his next move. He called Brenda and asked her if she was ready for him and Mr. Robinson to come over for his analysis of the ruby.

"That's fine" she responded, "Come over anytime."

Ralph goes directly to his office at the agency to talk with Toby about the latest developments. When he enters the office, his nose was greeted with the aromatic aroma of Toby's pipe tobacco, which he loved to smell.

"Sit down and grab a cup of coffee," Toby told him as he stripped off his coat.

"I've got some good news for you," Ralph began as he sat down at Toby's desk.

"Brenda has given me the OK to bring Mr. Robinson to the house with me to examine the ruby that Spaulding gave to his mother."

"Mr. Robinson?" Toby asked.

"Yeah, He's the gemologist that Bob recommended to me.

"So he's the one that Bob mentioned to me."

"I hate to say this, but we'll have to wait until Brenda's mom passes away before we can do anything else. That feels a little earie just waiting for someone to die." Ralph remarked.

"I understand," Toby said sympathetically "but sometimes death is a blessing, especially for someone in her condition. Nobody wants to linger and suffer, and become a burden on their loved ones."

"Thanks, I needed that," Ralph replied.

"When do you and Robinson plan to make your visit?"

"I told Brenda tomorrow around noon.

The next morning, Ralph goes to Robinson's office with a knot in the pit of his stomach, from anticipation of the upcoming events. Toby's words from yesterday did help to make him feel a little better about what he had to do at Brenda's. The two decided to ride together in Robinson's car as a safeguard from arousing any suspicion, just in case an unexpected visitor dropped by to see Brenda's mother.

"Nobody has any idea what this ruby looks like," Ralph begins, "All we know is that it was priced to sell for around Thirty thousand at Monsero's jewelry store before it was stolen."

"No one knows the size, color or type of ruby?"

"No nothing at all! That's why you are so important to our investigation."

"Mr. Smith has hired our agency to recover it, and is willing to pay the price to get it back, so it must be extremely important to him

"If it's priced at thirty thousand dollars, it must be a valuable piece of jewelry."

When they arrived at Brenda's, Ralph rang the doorbell, and Brenda soon answered.

"I'm very glad to see you and your guest," she says giving Ralph a warm hug. Please come in."

Ralph and Robinson were soon seated and served with a hot cup of coffee.

"Both of us are very sorry to hear about your mother" Ralph tells her.

"Thank you both" was her reply, "But it is what it is."

"Mr. Robinson here would like to take a look at the ruby your brother left."

"Of course," Brenda replied, standing up and disappearing into the room where her mother was. She soon reappeared with the ruby in tow. "Mother was sleeping and I didn't wake her. However, she did tell me earlier that she wanted to hear about the results of the analysis when it's finished."

What Ralph saw made him gasp!

What Brenda carried in her hand was without a doubt the biggest and most beautiful gem he had ever seen. It was big enough to almost cover the palm of her tiny hand, and was the richest and most robust red color that Ralph had ever seen. He had seen ruby's before, but none as big or colorful as this one.

When Brenda handed Robinson the ruby, the very first thing he did was to emit an audible whistle of surprise with wide eyes. He turned it over and over again in his hand, seemingly savoring everything he saw. He then pulled out a magnifying glass and donned a pair of special spectacles from his suit pocket, and began turning the ruby over in his hands several times, and examining it with the utmost of intensity.

After what seemed like an eternity, he finally said that the ruby was one of the world's most valued gems, an Heirloom ruby which are were worth millions.

"How much did you say that this was selling for?"

"Thirty thousand dollars" Ralph said.

"It's worth at least three times that amount or more" Robinson exclaimed.

"Ralph responded with an audible whistle of disbelief, and Brenda nearly fainted.

"But wait! That's not that's not the half of it." Robinson continued." This is a cut from a larger piece. It's only a part of the original, and cut very professionally I might add."

"What are you saying Mr. Robinson?" Ralph asked him in disbelief. Brenda was too stunned to respond at all.

"This is only a small piece of a larger Heirloom ruby undoubtedly worth millions."

"How can you tell? Ralph asked.

"By the way that the cut was made, and how the size was reduced from the whole. This was done by cutting experts, in a most admirable fashion. It had been deburred slightly as not to leave any sharp cutting edges, truly a most masterful work of art. Fantastic!" Robinson uttered.

There was a silence in the room that was deafening. Brenda and Ralph could not believe what they were hearing. Brenda was advised not to tell her mother of Mr. Robinson's finding, but just to leave things as they are for the time being.

"If this ruby is that valuable, why would Mr. Smith sell it so cheaply?" Ralph asked.

"I don't know, you'll have to ask him," was Robinson's reply.

"Brenda, under no circumstances, let no one know what Mr. Robinson has just told us. The average person who looks at this ruby would have no clue as to what they were looking at."

"I know, just like us."

"Wait until Toby hears about this," Ralph whispered half aloud to himself more than to anyone else.

Afterwards before leaving, Brenda served them hot coffee and cookies. She was still visibly shaken.

"It didn't take a rocket scientist to notice there was something drastically wrong, when I first saw this ruby that Hank had given to mother."

"When you called and told me of your suspicions, I can certainly understand why now." Ralph said.

After leaving Brenda's house heading back to the office, Robinson mentioned how impressed he was with Brenda's cooperation and hospitality.

"Yeah, she's a special person," Ralph replied.

"Is she married?"

"No, I don't believe so,"

"Hmm" Robinson remarked.

Ralph could not remember when he was so excited about anything. This was a monumental breakthrough in their investigation, and he couldn't wait until he got back. He was extremely impressed with Robinson and his demeanor, as well as his expertise. Bob was to be commended for his recommendation. When they finally arrived back at the office, Ralph thanked Robinson for all of his input, and dashed into the office to meet with Toby, who immediately observed his excitement and body language.

"I can tell that you have some exciting news to share with me.

"Boy, do I have"

"Tell me what happened"

"Well, you're not going to believe this," Ralph began, "But the gemologist's analysis' of the ruby was mindboggling.

"How so, what made it so significant?" Toby inquired.

"Well, for starters, the ruby we have is only part of the world's most valuable and expensive kind of Gem, an Heirloom ruby, and the piece we have is only a part of a whole."

"Whoa. What do you mean only a part?"

"Our ruby was cut out of a much larger block. Robinson examined the shape and size of our ruby, and determined that it was cut out of the original block, by a team of expert cutters into its present size. He estimated that the whole original ruby was probably worth several hundred thousand"

"Good Lord" Toby exclaimed, "I had no idea that rubies could be so expensive."

"According to Robinson, they are one of the world's most precious stones."

After letting the information settle in for a few minutes, the two settled back in their chairs to digest it all, and Toby took the time to light his pipe.

"The fact that Smith was selling the ruby for only thirty thousand is an indication that he too had no idea of it's true worth."

"That's right" Toby replied, "Which leads me to wonder why not."

Ralph could notice the look of puzzlement on Toby's face, and could almost hear the wheels in his head turning.

"What's going on?" he asked.

"I need an answer to that question, and the only way for me to get it is to talk to Smith, and find out who he bought the ruby from, and for how much."

"How can the rest of the gang help you at this point?"

"With this new information, I need to call James and John, and let them know I'll need to call the group together in order to determine where we need to go from here."

"That's sounds reasonable enough."

After Ralph's departure, Toby calls James and John, who were also as mesmerized by this new information as he was.

"This raises a whole host of other questions that needs to be examined." James concluded.

"I'd be interested to know what Bob and police will think." John wondered aloud.

"We'll soon find out" Toby replied.

"We'll have the boys released to rejoin you, so that you can best determine your next move as a group."

"Right" Toby responded. "A lot of it will depend on what happens when Hank Spaulding makes his next move."

When their conversation ended, Toby called Bob at headquarters to bring him up to date.

Bob agreed with Toby's assessment of his interview with Smith about the nature of the purchase of the ruby and the seller.

"There's a couple avenues that need to be explored with this new information." He suggested. "One is that this suggests a bigger theft than we at first realized, which is something that our department needs to investigate, and secondly if our assistance is needed in any area, we'll assigned Dick to work with your group."

"What are you thinking this all means then?" Toby asked.

"Well, with what you mentioned about Smith apparently not knowing the true value of the ruby, and the information about it being a part of a larger rock, gives both of us something to work on. Our department will do a worldwide search to try and find out if a larger theft took place somewhere, that our ruby may be a part of, in order to get it returned to its rightful owner."

"And in the meantime, "Toby added, "I'm going to be working with Smith about his purchase of the ruby and who he bought it from. Wow! It looks like we've opened up Pandora's box."

"It certainly looks that way" Bob surmised.

"Well, so goes the nature of investigative work. You never know what might turn up" Bob said.

"Exactly what I told our guys a little while back during their investigative work" was Toby's reply.

Toby's first task after finishing his conversations with, James, John and Bob, Was to contact Monteros jewelry store and set up an appointment with Smith. He called him on the phone.

"I think it's become necessary for me to examine your books, and talk to you about the person you bought the ruby from."

"What brought this all about?"

"Since the last time we Talked, several significant events have taken place which turns our investigation in this direction. We'll need to sit down together."

"OK, just tell me when."

"What about noon tomorrow?"

"Sounds like a plan."

"Good. See you then."

Toby's next goal was to get his staff together for a group meeting and discussion of their next move.

After talking to them, he sat back smoking his pipe, and reviewing everything up to now. The latest developments came completely unexpected, and had shifted everything. His other private investigations would have to be altered in order to accommodate these newest developments.

When all of the staff had been assembled in the investigation room, Toby greeted them and pulled out his chalk board.

"This is where we are now in our investigation. We now have at least three separate investigations going on at the same. Number one he writes on the board is the work with Bob and the police department to try and find out if the ruby we have is connected to a larger robbery somewhere else in the world, in light of what Ralph's work with the gemologist who examined the ruby at Hank Spaulding's mother's house who is dying from cancer."

"This is all news to us," Rodney said.

"I know," Toby acknowledged, I'll explain it all as we go. The second phase is the examination of Mr. Smith's books, because I think he was deceived with the purchase of his ruby. He writes this as number two on the board.

"Thirdly, we have to wait on Spaulding to go his mother's to retrieve the ruby after she dies, in order to have him arrested and to establish his hidden motives. He entered this as the third item on the board.

"It's now time to hear your questions about all of this."

"First let's back up to number one" Jeremy said. What is all this about an internal investigation by the police department about another robbery?"

"When Ralph and a jewelry expert examined the ruby that Hank Spaulding had given to this dying mother, it was determined that the thirty thousand dollar asking price that Smith had listed the ruby to sell for, was at least three times less than what the true value of it.

"You mean that the ruby we have is really worth at least ninety thousand?"

"That's right."

"Good grief!" Jeremy exclaimed, followed ny a similar response from the others.

"Then why would Smith list it at only thirty thousand?"

"That's what I've got to find out" Toby answered.

"And you'll find that out by asking Smith who he bought the ruby from and what he was told it was worth." Dick said.

"Exactly, otherwise why would he undersell it so significantly?" another asked.

"If he thought that this was a reasonable selling price, why would he be so determined to absorb the cost of finding it?"

"I don't know that either. This still gives us no clue as to his real motives are behind getting it back. This question has always been nagging at me, his motives."

"So this leaves us in a holding pattern for the time being" Rod concluded. "We have to wait for the police's work to be done, as well as Toby's work to finish with Smith.'

"Which leaves us at number three on the board, Ralph's work with Spaulding's family, the police, and his subsequent arrest once he's caught" Jeremy said.

"Tell us what the plan is" asked Rod.

"Bob is preparing to get a search warrant for Spaulding's house, a warrant for his arrest once the ruby is in his possession, with it to remain in the custody of the police, until information comes in about its possible connection if any, with another robbery." Ralph answered.

"Are there any more questions or observations from anyone else?" Toby asked the group before bringing the meeting to a close. Hearing nothing else, he closed the meeting with the final instruction for everyone to wait until they hear back from him. As far as the work left to do for them to do was now over.

Everything was now left in the hands of Ralph and Toby to persue.

Toby went to Smith's office at the time they agreed to meet, and was greeted by Smith at the door.

"It's good to see you again, Toby." Smith said.

"Same here," responded Toby, "I would have preferred different circumstances though."

"I'm eaten up with curiosity as to the events that make this visit necessary."

"That's completely understandable. Let me start at the beginning. First of all our agency knows where your ruby is."

Smith was floored by Toby's words.

"You actually know where my ruby is?" he said in wide eyed disbelief.

"Yes, but we don't have it yet, or the man. Until the police know who stole it, and the person who did, they can't close the case. The man we suspect has yet to be connected to the thieves and the robbery. This is what the police are working on now."

"First of all, we had a gemologist examine your ruby, one of the best experts available, and it was

Determined that your ruby is actually worth at least **ninety** thousand dollars, and was cut from a larger stone down to its present size."

"Did you say ninety thousand dollars?" He asked unbelievably.

"That's right."

"I need a drink" Smith murmured, staggering out of his chair. "Can I offer you one?" he asked Toby.

"No thanks," Toby responded, "Not while I'm duty, but I will have a cup of coffee, cream and sugar" and added that hoped it would be OK to smoke his pipe.

"Yes, yes, do whatever you want. I need time to take all of this in."

"I know the feeling very well," Toby said. "When I heard this news, I was shocked to say the least."

Smith went over to the desk in the corner of the room, and retrieved a bottle from one of the drawers, picked up a glass from the wall cabinet, put in some ice cubes, and poured him a drink. He went into the adjoining office told his secretary to pour Toby some coffee. When she returned, the two men settled back in their chairs. After a few minutes to relax again, Toby resumed his conversation.

"If you know where my ruby is, why can't you just go and get?"

"I can't say at this point because the investigation is still ongoing."

"When can I expect to get it?"

"Once the case is closed.because of the true value of the ruby, and the information surrounding it, the police will conduct a national search to see if it may be connected to a robbery somewhere."

"This is all so unbelievable."

"Once we found out the value of the ruby, it became apparent that either you purposely underpriced the ruby for sale, or did not know what it's true worth was."

"I can assure you that I did not undervalue the price of the ruby."

"Then he must have had a reson for deceiving you."

"But why would he do that?"

"That's what the police and I want to find out."

"What do you know about the guy who sold you the ruby?"

"I met him over a year ago at an international convention in Cairo, and he was one of the jewelers there that I talked to. He seemed like a very nice guy at we hit it off pretty well."

"Well, we question his integrity and honesty, and believe you might have been duped."

"This makes me feel like a fool."

"Bob at headquarters has asked me to get the name and address of the person you purchased the ruby from, so they can investigate where the rest of it is. They suspect that it couldhave been part of a robbery and the person who sold it to you, may have been a fence of stolen contraband, and might have sold it because it was hot. They won't know this until their investigation is complete."

"This is all absolutely unbelievable," Smith uttered again.

Toby waited a minite or two to allow Smith to regain his composure.

"Give me a moment and I'll go and get this man's name, address and phone number, as well as the receipt he gave me for the sale."

"Great" Toby replied.

After what seemed like an eternity, Smith returned with all of the information Toby asked for. He then had his secretary make a copy of everything, and handed them to Toby.

"I'll keep you informed and up to date on everything," Toby told him before leaving the store.

"Thank you very much," Smith responded, "I really do appreciate that."

After leaving, Toby couldn't help but feel a little sorry for Smith who was visibly crestfallen and deflated. Here was an honest, hardworking man, who fell victim to a scheme that he felt was too tempting to pass up. Toby immediately called Bob and gve him an update of his meeting with Smith.

"I'll bring the information you asked for to your office before the day is through."

"Solid!" Bob exclaimed."We'll keep you and your group up to date on our investigation."

"Good enough, I'll make sure that James and John stay informed."

Toby spent the next several minutes wracking his brain about where he could go from here. All bases were covered as far he could see. Smith's books and records were scrutinized to his satisfaction, he was preparing to take the name and address of the person that Smith bought the ruby from to Bob, as well as waiting to hear from him about the next phase of their plan for Spaulding's capture. He was satisfied that all of the bases were covered and that all he needed was to wait until he hears from the police, and Ralph.He was at a standstill for the time time being. Contented for now, he left his office enroute to police headquarters and Bob's office.

Several weeks have now passed uneventfully, since he gave Bob the information he wanted, and his investigation and talk with Smith. Ralph and Karen in the meantime had developed a very deep relationship between them. Ralph still was having some difficulty accepting the fact that he had indeed fallen in love, and Karen was equally smitten. They had attended several more football games together, and always did so with the rest of the guys.

Today, they spent the evening together after Ralph finished his work at the chemical plant, where he was experimenting with a new chemical formula that worked as an adhesive, but was also removable without destroying what it was bonded to.They were lounging comfortably on her sofa, and he wanted to make love to her in the worst way.

"I'm an old fashioned girl as you know by now. My mother raised me that way about sex and some other things."

"What are you trying to say?" Ralph asked wryly.

"You know very well what I mean."

"I know, I know" he conceded. "I think its time for me to ask you a very significant question."

"And that is?" Karen asked also wryly.

"I think it's time that we get married. Karen, will you be my wife?"

"You don't need to ask" she answered. "Of course.I've been waiting for you to ask."

"Fantastic!" Ralph exclaimed. "I can't wait to spread the news. It's just been several months that we've known each other, but I felt like this from the the very time that I met you. Rod was right when he told me about love at first sight. I know that I'm going to be razzed about this unmercifully by the guys."

They both laughed together with tears running down their cheeks

"This calls for a celebration" Ralph said excitedly.

Karen agreed, and went to the kitchen to get a bottle of wine that she always kept handy. They celebrated together until both were tipsy.

"We'd better stop now before we go any further" Karen said beginning to feel like Ralph, sporting a raging hard on in his jeans. He reluctantly agreed with her.

Ralph received a phone call from Brenda the next day. When he heard her voice, he was overwhelmed with excitement. This news was exactly what he wanted to hear. On top of what happened yesterday between him and Karen, he was more excited than he could ever remember when Brenda called.

"Ralph, I'm calling because Hospice just said that mother is in her final stages of death, and that we should notify all of our family members to come as soon as possible."

"Brenda, I'm really sorry to hear that, but at the same time I feel a sense of peace that your mother's suffering in coming to an end."

"I know exactly what you're saying. I've been torn betweenfeelings of sadness and pain, and at the same time feelings of grief and peace."

"Where does the rest of your family live?"

"Hank and I don't have a big family, but what's left is spread out over the country. It will probably take at least sevweal days for them to all get here."

"How long did Hospice say she has left?"

"Just a couple of days, she asked me for her ruby the other day, and I gave it to her early this morning. She was barely conscious and awfully feeble. I've already called my brother and the rest of the family. Hank said that he is coming as soon as mother s is unconscience, or when the rest of the family is here, which ever comes first."

"You and your family certainly have our prayers."

"Thanks, Ralph, we can certainly use them. Tell me what you want me to do next."

"All you have to do is call me when he gets the ruby and heads for home. I don't to burden you with anything else at a time like this. You have enough to contend with."

"That's very thoughtful of you, Ralph. I know how important this is to you. "I'll call you as soon as mother is gone."

"I don't care what time of day or night it is. Just call."

"I will, I promise."

As soon as his conversation with Brenda was finished, Ralph immediately called Toby and relayed the news to him."

"Fantastic" Toby replied very excited and relieved. "This will finally let us move on to the next phase of our operation. "I'll need to make several phone calls and have James and John send the crew back to the office."

"Oh, by the way, Karen and I are engaged and will soon be married."

"Good grief, Ralph, you're full of good news and surprises today."

Toby settled back in his chair, and lit his pipe. This is the best that he has felt in weeks. He smoked leisurely on his pipe, thinking about the news that he had just heard before making his calls. This always served to relax and quiet him. His heart raced with excitement as the last piece of the puzzle seemed to be falling into place. Every thing from here on out will be left to Bob and his staff.

"Here's our plan" Bob tells Toby.

"When Spaulding retrieves the ruby following his mother's death, my crew and I will set up a twenty four hour surveillance of his home with unmarked cars. I'll get a search warrant and an arrest warrant while my men track his every move. Once we get the ruby, we'll keep it here at headquarters while we check to see if it may be connected with another robbery somewhere. Based on the report of the gemologist, I suspect that it may be."

"I'll have another talk with Smith when this happens just to keep him abreast of everything."

"Good, that also reminds me. When all of this is done, I think that I will begin planning to send Dick to Cairo with the ruby, and maybe give to the local authorities there, if this guy who sold it to Smith fails to cooperate.I would also like for him to take Rod or Jeremy from your company with him, since we're all working together on this. I don't want Dick to travel alone with such an expensive piece of merchandise. Like I said before, I think this guy is a fence of stolen goods and may have taken Smith for a ride."

"I feel bad for Smith because he's a hard working business man who just made a foolish, but careless mistake. I just hope that at least we may be able to get his twenty thousand dollars back for him." Toby said.

"Well, thanks for this latest info," Bob told Toby. "We're on it."

Toby called James and John the next day to share with them of the progress made, and what the future plans were.

"I have to say that you and your crew have made unbelievable progress on this case recently, both James and I are very impressed."

"We're only doing what you pay us to do, and what you expect in return."

"Very well put," James says, "Just let us know if you need anything at all."

Toby spent the rest of the day turning everything over in his mind, to make sure that nothing was overlooked. He could find nothing, and settled down in his chair before heading for home to share everything with Peg, and then have a good home cooked meal. He was famished for some reason or other and couldn't wait for her dinner.

He was especially shocked at the plans of Ralph to get married, and would talk with Peg about planning something special for the occasion. She was very good at that kind of thing, and he was very poor at it. He couldn't wait to see the reaction of the guys when the announcement is made at their next meeting. Other than dealing with the excitement of the upcoming events in the case, he was very contented and relaxed. New York was not so bad afterall, once you got used to it. Peg had now learned her way around, and now often went shopping by herself.

Toby's thoughts were interrupted when his phone rang. It was Ralph. Brenda's mother had just died. Ralph immediately got Brenda on the phone.

"Brenda I'm so sorry tohear about your mother. How are you doing?"

"I'm OK, thanks for asking. I'm just glad it's over, and surprised that I feel this great sense of calm and relief."

"That's because you had become accustomed to taking care of your mom, and had learned to live with that pressure. You'd be surprised at how much that takes out of a person."

"I know you're right. You're the first person that I've called, and my brother Hank will be the next. I expect to see him tomorrow when mom's pastor comes to the house to be with every body. We've all been expecting this for a while, so we'll be all right."

"That's good to hear.When Hank comes and leaves your house to go home, call and let me know. OK?"

"I will."

"I'll let you go now. You have a million things to do and phone calls to make."

"I'll call you as soon as Hank leaves. Thanks for calling me back."

"OH. By the way, my gemologist who appraised the value of your mom's ruby thought that you were extremely attractive, and wanted to know if you married. I told that you were single as far as I know. He'll probably be calling you if that's OK."

"That'll be fine."

"Good! I'll let him know."

When their conversation was over, Ralph immediately called Toby to give him the news. His heart was racing so fast that it felt like it going to come out of his chest. Toby received the news with great excitement.

Ralph, I want to tell you what a fantastic job I think you've done with all this. I could'nt have done it better myself. This finally brings us to the brink of solving this case. I'll call Bob right away with this information, to give his sufficient time to get all of his ducks in a row."

When Toby called Bob, he was even more excited than he was. Toby smiled broadly to himself at Bob's enthusiasm.

"The first thing that needs to be done, is to set up the undercover surveillance crew at Spaulding's house, and then get the warrants that I need to finish this. Man, am I pumped" he finished.

"Me too" Toby responded, his heart racing.

Toby goes over to the cabinet next to his desk, when he had finished talking to Bob, and poured himself a drink, and settled down in his chair to relax and light his pipe. Everything was now left up to Bob and his men to finish. He felt a great sense of satisfaction with everything surrounding this case. His agency was about to recover the missing ruby that no one seemed to know nothing about, and the police were close to apprehending the last of the theives in order to close the books on the robbery.

Bob called all of his men together to formulate the plans to apprehend Spaulding, after he had obtained the necessary documents from a judge to search his house and make the arrest.

"When do we make our move?" one of the men asked.

"We will need to give him enough time to get in his house with the ruby, before we make our move. We have the search warrant so there's no need to rush. I'll give the signal when to make our move. Every body will be in street clothes while we sit in our vehicles. We'll wait for Ralph's call before we do anything."

Brenda calls Ralph the next morning to tell him that the family was beginning to arrive and that Hank had come earlier to get the ruby.

"I told him that it was in the top drawer of the nightstand next to momma's bed. He got it immediately and then left after a very brief greeting with the rest of the family. They never did get along together for whatever reason."

"How long ago did he leave?"

"He left probably about fifteen minutes or so."

"Are you OK?"

"I'm hanging in there. The minister will be coming soon to console the family. I need to get busy rounding up all of the insurance papers for the funeral home."

"Let me know if there's anything that I can do."

"I will, and thanks for everything." Brenda concluded as the call ended.

ImmediatelyRalph called Bob.

"I'll wait an hour or so before I send in my men. I'm releasing one agent as we speak, to go to Spaulding's house immediately for early surveillance."

Bob's heart was racing with anticipation and relief. Finally! At long last the end may be in sight for the closing of this case. He owed a great deal to Reliford Investigations and their work. He deserved a pat on the back for formulating the coalition with them.

After notifying Bob, Ralph immediately called to brief Toby.

"It looks like the last piece is in place and the dye has been cast." Toby remarked.

"That's something that I've never heard before" Ralph said.

"Oh, that's an old engineering term meaning that the sand mold is formed in which to pour in the molten steel to make a permanent metal part."

"That's a neat expression, andIt certainly looks that way. I'm so excited that I don't know what to do." Ralph said.

"Me too, that's because we've worked so hard to bring this moment to pass.

When Bob's agent arrived at Spaulding's house, he was just getting out of his car and heading for the front door.

"I've got him pegged" he tells Bob on the car phone.

"Great," Bob responds. "Keep him in your sights at all times, and never lose him. If he leaves the house for any reason, follow him, and if anyone comes to the house, get a make on the vehicle, and a description of the person, and call me right away."

"You got it, boss," he replied.

After a brief period, a vehicle arrives at the house, and the agent immediately calls Bob. He gives him the make of the vehicle, a description of the man who went into the house.

"I'll run a check on him right away." Bob responds.

Bob discovers that the man is a known jewelry expert.

"He's probably there to assess the value of the ruby," Bob tells the detective. "Spaulding doesn't have the information we have about it. When he leaves, we'll make our arrest."

"Gotcha." The agent responded.

When the man leaves the house, Bob receives the call from his agent, and orders his men to go immediately to Spaulding's, and wait to see if anyone else comes to the house. He then calls Toby.

"I'm thinking maybe somebody to pawn the ruby on now that he knows what its worth" he tells Toby.

"That makes a lot of sense to me."

"I'm calling in my men to make the arrest now."

"OK" Toby acknowleged. "Good luck."

Bob's men move in.

"Mr. Spaulding. The police" they tell him when he answers the door, displaying their ID's.

"What's this all about?" he exclaimed in obvious shock.

"We have a search warrant, so stand aside" Sgt. Blake said roughly pushing his way inside.

"A search warrant for what?" said an agitated Spaulding.

"Can the crap Spaulding" he told him, as his men entered the house and began their search.

"We know you have the missing ruby, and as soon as we find it you're going to jail. I also have this." He said showing Spaulding the arrest warrant.

The police searched diligently for several minutes without success.

"I told you I don't know what you're talking about," said a defiant Spaulding.

The search continued for many more minutes without finding anything.

"Tell me where the ruby is, or I'll have my men tear your house apart, piece by piece."

"Do what you want" Spaulding shot back.

"Hey boss," one of Blake's men said, "look at this behind the picture."

Blake went over to a picture which was hiding a safe behind it in the wall.

"Very cleaver.So this is where the ruby is. Open it up or we'll open it for you,"

Reluctantly, Spaulding opened up the safe, and a deputy pulled out the ruby.

"Holy cow!" he said in disbelief. "Look at this, fellas."

The other officers gawked in disbelief, at the astounding magnificent piece.

"I've never seen anything like it," one uttered in disbelief.

They all passed the ruby around for each one to see, all with wide eyes of disbelief.

"I can now see what all of the excitement is about this piece" Blake acknowlwdged.

"Put the cuffs on him and lets him downtown.

Blake calls Bob and tells him that they are enroute.

"Great!" was Bob's only response, as they loaded Spaulding into one of the cars.

Once they arrived at headquarters, Spaulding was fingerprinted and photograghed.

"What's the charge?" he demanded.

"Possesion of stolen goods,' Bob told him, as the officer read him his rights.

"I have no idea what you mean by stolen. I found this ruby in a vacant lot on the ground."

Everyone in the room snickered.

"Right, you just happened to stumble upon something like this in a field somewhere?"

"That's right, just like that."

"And where was this so called field located?"

"I'm not answering anything else without an attorney. I know that you're aware of the Miranda rights." He stated beligerantly.

Bob was agitated with his haughty and almost mocking attitude. He was also a little troubled, because eventhough they had him dead to rights and knew he was guilty,, all they had was an abundance of circumstantial evidence, and Spaulding seemed to know that. This was one of the things that frustrated Bob. You work hard to do your job, and because of a technicality it could all be in jeopardy.

They would either have to prove that he was in on the theft, orlet him go. That thought almost made him sick. They led Spaulding to a holding cell in the jail portion of the building, where they detained prisoners temporarily until a lawyer was notified. It contained only a commode, sink, cot, and a faucet.

He stretched out on the cot and asked one of the guards for a cigarette. He was given one by a jail guard who knew nothing about the criminal investigation. The guard later wished that he had not given him one, once he became aware of the circumstances. While he smoked the cigarette, an attorney was ushered in to his cell. When he entered, he addressed Spaulding in a matter-of-fact tone.

"I understand that you are being held on possession of stolen contraband."

"Yeah, so they so, but I have no idea what they mean by stolen."

"Then why would they bring such a charge?"

"Because they're trying to link me with the gang that robbed Monsero's Jewelry store a little while ago."

"What evidence do they have to justify their claim?"

"They locked me up for having a ruby I found while jogging in a field which they say was stolen. I don't know anything about a missing ruby being stolen. I gave it to my mother who is dying. That's all I know."

"You do know that they plan to have you arraigned before a judge on criminal charges?"

"I figured as much."

"How do you plan to plea?"

"Since I don't know what they're talking about, what do you recommend?"

"Enter the Alfred Plea."

"And what is the Alfred Plea?"

"It's a plea of not being innocent or guilty, which leaves the burden of proof on the prosection."

"Then that's the way I'm going."

"Very good," his attorney tells him," I will let them know."

Once Bob received this information, he was a little perturbed and uneasy, because this plea was often difficult.

"Damn it," he uttered to one of his men. "It's as if a strong case of circumstantial evidence is irrelevant. I don't think they understand just how much work is required to get it sometime.

"I know it's frustrating" one of his officers said sympathetically.

"When will the arraignment take place?" Spaulding in the meantime wanted to know.

"That all depends on when the judge hears your case."

"Can I be released to go home until that time?"

"I'm afraid not. They can hold a person for at least three days just on suspicion. Just sit tight, I'll be in touch"

Spaulding reclined back on the cot after the lawyer left, feeling not as confident as did before, but still hopeful. Knowing that he would be interrogated again by the police, luckily for him, all that they had to go on was their suspicions.

"You know we've got you by the balls" Bob told him in the interrogation room.

"Why, just because you know that I had the ruby?"

"Because it was stolen"

"I didn't know that. Can you prove that I did?"

"Not yet, but we will." Bob said slamming his fist on the table angrily.

"Well, until you do all of this is unnecessary."

Two days later, Bob receives word that the judge will hear Spauding's Case.Bob was elated. Spaulding was taken out of his cell, and escorted, not too kindly, to the judge's chamber along with the officers. The judge began by telling them that the purpose of this meeting.

This arraignment is simply to examine the charges and credibility of them against this man, and to determine if further action is needed."

"We understand your honor," acknowledged Bob.

He then read them all back to Bob.

"I have read the charges in detail against Mr. Spaulding here, and just need confirmation that all I've read to you is correct and accurate."

"Yes it is your honor."

"I'm convinced that your findings are convincing to you and your department, but need I remind you that it is all circumstantial, regardless of the amount of it you have. The jury will still have to be convinced at the pre- trial."

Bob and his companions all nodded their heads in agreement.

"Mr. Spaulding, aside from your claim of innocence, is the information submitted to me correct?"

"Yes it is your honor."

"Then this arraignment is over, and I'll set a date for the pre- trial to begin"

This was music to Bob's ears. He and his colleagues celebrated the decision of the judge hear the case, and to begin the proceeding for a pre-trial. He was confident of the case against Spaulding, even if it was only circumstantial.

The next step was to wait for the judge's decision to set the pre-trial date. Bob's next step was to give the news of the judge's decision to Toby. Toby was talking to a client when his phone rang.

"Toby you busy?"

"Hey Bob. I'm with a client right now, but I've always got time for you. What's up?""

"Let me get back with you when you're free. I've got some information that I'm sure you'll be glad to hear. Call me when you're ready."

"I will" Toby responded his heart racing with excitement. Bob never calls him unless he has some vital information to pass on.

After completing the conference with his client, Toby returns Bob's call.

"You'd better begin to get your crew together. I just finished meeting with the district judge about an arraignment of Spaulding, and he decided to have a pre-trial, to determine whether or not Spaulding can be tried with the evidence we've presented."

"Explain" Toby requested.

"Well, what it means is that the judge will hand down an indictment against Spaulding to stand a pre-trial investigation, to determine his guilt or innocence, without a jury present. This will determine whether his case will be bound over to a grand jury."

"Wow! That's fantastic," Toby bellowed, dropping his pipe in his excitement.

"Yeah, I thought you'd like that," bob remarked with a grin, "Finally we're going somewhere."

"I know, but it's going to be an uphill battle all the way. Spaulding is still declaring his innocence and is using the Alfred Plea at the advice of his attorney."

"We all expected that, but the judge was in agreement, that what we have is enough to warrant a case against him. As soon as I receive word about the date of the pre-trial, I'll call you right away."

"I'll be waiting." Toby responded'

Toby, his investigation agency and James and John were all exuberant at the news, to say the least. This is what they've all been waiting for.

"We have to spread the news that the fifth member of the gang who robbed the jewelry store has been indicted to stand trial." James said.

"As soon as word is received about the pre-trial, we'll start the publicity." John agreed. "What a tremendous opportunity for our enterprise and Reliford Investigations."

"I'm pumped," James added. "If people were impressed with the press and publication about the boys standing trial in midway last year, and their release to return to school at Wayne State, they haven't seen anything like what we will do with this." James added.

"For sure," John continued. "Toby, if you think we made you a hero last year, just wait and see what's going to happen with this."

Toby was speechless. He remembered how he was received here in the Bronx upon him and Peg's arrival, and the reception by everyone connected with the university and their friends,, he could only imagine what it would be like this time, especially since he lives here.

"This calls for a celebration" James exclaimed, popping the cork on a bottle of champaign he got from the office refrigerator.

"You got that right" John agreed.

What more could a man ask for than by having a bottle of champaign with his bosses as celebration of a job well done, Toby was thinking to himself smiling broadly. It just didn't get any better than this. He would now get to see first hand how James and John went about doing their work.

CHAPTER FIVE

OB SAT IN HIS OFFICE at police headquarters, waiting anxiously for the judge's decision about the indictment of Spaulding. His superiors were waiting just as anxiously because they wanted this case to end. The public was clamoring for an end and the prosecution of all the thieves involved. Even the mayor had become involved.

"Have you heard anything yet," the district attorney, Mario Denton, asked him, passing by his office door.

"Nothing yet," Bob told him.

This went on for a couple more days, until Bob's office phone rang.

"Bob, this is Judge Terrance McGill. I've set a date for Spaulding's pre-trial. I'm satisfied with the information you presented to me and it's sufficient enough to warrant a pre-trial.

Bob wanted to shout with joy, but contained his enthusiasm.

"I see," he responded very professionally.

"I've set the date for two weeks from today at nine O'clock AM."

"That's fantastic," your honor, I will notify everybody involved."

For the next several hours, he busied himself on the phone, notifiying everyone about the news.

"Finally!" the chief of police said to Bob.

"Well, it's time to go to work," was John's response when he received the word from Bob. Their first step was to draft a memo saying exactly what they wanted to convey, and then notify all of the contributing newspapers in the area, about the date of the pre-trial.

The first thing they wanted to notify the public about was that this is only a pre-trial, to determine whether or not an indictment would be handed down by the judge. It would not be a trial by jury. Even so, with all the public concern and outcry over the robbery, any news would be received with open arms. The process was now begun, with every newspaper struggling to be the first to break the news. The news the next day had the whole town abuzz with excitement, and anticipation. Smith and Montero's braced themselves for the onslaught. If there was anyone who had never heard of them before, that was all about to change.

Toby and his agency relished the opportunity for the publicity. Just as it would be for Montero's, the same would be true Reliford Investigations. Toby's client load had already begun to grow as word spread about his work, now it would probably mushroom.

Wingate Enterprise would probably be the biggest recipient of it all, being the sponsoring agent of Reliford Investigations, and several other businesses, while being the leading organization in the area, would only bring them more notoriety.

This was a win, win situation for everyone involved.

The municipal courtroom was crammed with spectators and reporters. An almost carnival atmosphere existed as to the high level of anticipation. This robbery was almost exclusively the talk of the city since it happened, and now that the missing thief had been apprehended by police, his pre-trial was front page news on every paper in town. Many people had already chosen sides about whether or not an indictment would be handed down,

Judge Terrence McGill felt it necessary maintain absolute control over the upcoming proceedings, because of the level of excitement and anticipation this case had caused. He spoke in a deliberate and measured manner.

"First of all this is a pretrial, not a jury trial. No indictment has been handed down at this point. That is the purpose of this proceeding. We are here only to ascertain whether or not the prosecution has sufficient evidence to warrant charges against Mr. Spaulding. I will tolerate no disturbances or interruptions from any onlookers at any time or I'll clear the courtroom. I will hear the evidence presented and will render my judgement at the trial's conclusion."

The judge's remarks brought an instant hush over the buzzing courtroom. It was if everyone present was holding their breath at the same time. You could literally hear a pin drop. After a brief pause and being satisfied that he had accomplished the end result he desired. Judge McGill continued.

"Are both the counsels for the prosecution and the defense in the courtroom at this time?"

The prosecuting attorney for Bob, Dale Forsyth, and Mark Blunden, the defense attorney for Spaulding both stood. The judge nodded and they both sat down.

"Is the defendant present in the courtroom?"

Hank Spaulding stood up. When he was acknowledged, he sat down.

"Let's proceed then by hearing the prosecutor's opening argument." Dale Forsyth rose deliberately from his seat and strode confidently to the front of the courtroom. He was a tall, handsome and well-groomed man of 45 with sideburns that were grey at the temple. His dark blue suit was immaculate, highlighting the steel blueness of friendly, but penetrating eyes that scanned the courtroom. He was the epitome of professionalism that you would expect representing James and John. He had a reputation of being an astute and deadly trial lawyer, one who went directly for the jugular in his prosecution. His courtroom tactics were sometimes shrewed but never unethical. He was what is known as a 'hard hitter.'

The spectators watched his every move as he approached the bench to begin. His voice matched his appearance.

"Your honor, ladies and Gentlemen, the prosecution will produce evidence to warrant criminal charges of possessing stolen contraband, and a connection with the thieves who robbed Montero's jewelry store."

"Objection, your honor, all the prosecution has is circumstantial evidence."

"That's not entirely true, your honor. We have a combination of real and circumstantial evidence which points to the defendant's guilt."

"Objection overruled" the judge said. "Proceed with your presentation, attorney Forsyth."

"On the day of the robbery, Mr. Spaulding's car was seen by a witness sitting in the alley behind the store. It was determined later that it was the get-a-way car driven by Mr. Spaulding, who escaped detection inside the store during the robbery, because he was outside in the car waiting."

"That's pure speculation, your honor. Who made the determination? Nobody has identified my client as being involved including the thieves" Blunden argued.

"Our evidence proves otherwise," Forsyth countered. "Immediately after the crime was committed, the store's security guard found cigar butts on the ground behind the store, left by the defendant while he waited in the car during the robbery. The same cigar butts were also found in the ash tray of Spaulding's car by Reliford private investigators. They were matched by DNA to be the same as the one's found in the alley. That proves that the man in the car during the theft was the same man as the get-a-way driver."

Loud gasps of surprise were audible from the spectators, and the low buzz of whispering filled the courtroom. The judge rapped his gavel twice and silence once again ruled.

"As I said earlier, I will not tolerate disturbances in my court. Continue."

"Yes your honor," replied Blunden." You stated that the butts found proved that this man was the get-a-way driver. All it proves is that he could have been the driver, but that in itself is inconclusive. What makes you think that you can draw such a conclusion?"

"I'll accept that, but the likelihood of it being accurate, is more than can be dismissed as lightly as you are trying to do." Forsyth said angrily, pointing an accusing finger at his rival. He decided to take a calculated risk and test the judge's patience, because he saw the bantering between him and Blunden a stale mate.

"Don't point your finger at me," Blunden said vehemently.

"Order in the court," barked the judge" I want both of you here in front of me, before I charge you with contempt."

Forsyth smiled to himself as they approached the judge's bench. His risk had worked to his satisfaction.

In a hushed, but stern voice, the judge told them both that another outburst by either of them again would cause him to declare a mistrial.

They both nodded their heads in agreement.

"I understand where both of you are coming from," he tells them. "So far both of you make valid arguments, so let's continue in a civil manner."

Both attorneys agreed and went back to their benches. Forsyth was elated.

"If what you said is true that the butts found in the alley, and in my client's car were one and the same, then why wasn't he identified by the gang that robbed the store?" challenged Blunden.

"The criminal code of ethics, they never tell on one another."

"A criminal code of ethics?" chided Blunden.

"Come on! stop playing games with the public. You know full well as a lawyer, about their code of ethics they have. Why do think it took the FBI so long to crack the mafia and their mob leaders?"

"If they did not finger him, how do you expect us to believe that he was one of them?"

"That's what we're here to find out."

"Good luck and how are we supposed to do that when all you have is guess work and speculation."

"By the evidence we have placing him at the scene of the crime, finding his cigar butts there and also the same ones in his car. It's not guess work or speculation, its circumstantial evidence gathered by my investigators."

"That still doesn't prove a thing," shot Blunden at Forsyth.

Forsyth knew that a change of direction was needed here. This was getting him nowhere at this point.

"Well let's go to another piece of what you call circumstantial evidence. Can you explain how your client just happens to be in possession of a stolen ruby valued at over ninety thousand dollars?"

"No I can't" Blunden said" But how can you prove he stole it?"

"Then tell the court what your opinion is on the matter since you are representing him as his Attorney?"

"I can't do that either. You'll have to find that out for yourself."

"Then what do you know?" Forsyth asked sarcastically.

Laughter filled the courtroom. The judge pounded his gavel to restore order.

"Ask him yourself." Blunden responded pointing at his client.

"You know full well that he is not on the witness stand. You ask him as his attorney how he came into the possession of the stolen ruby."

Blunden confers briefly with his client privately in whispers then proceeds back to the podium.

"MY client refuses to answer the question on grounds that it might incriminate him."

"So he is pleading the fifth amendment?"

"Yes"

"He can't get away with that, it's just a simple question."

Blunden simply shrugged his shoulders.

"OK. Then ask him where it was that he found the ruby?"

Again, Spaulding and his attorney confer privately.

"His plea is still the same."

Forsyth then addresses the judge impatiently.

"Your honor, this is ridiculous. How can Mr. Blunden refuse to answer a simple question when there is nothing to incriminate him on, therefore I can only assume that he's hiding something?"

"I object you honor!" shouted Blunden. "The defense is drawing an unfound conclusion."

Again the courtroom is filled with noise and commotion.

"Yeah!" someone in the audience shouted loudly. "Answer the question, Spaulding."

Several other people voiced their agreement as well.

"Order in the court, order in the court "judge McGill barked angrily.

He loudly banged his gavel three times on his desk.

"This court is adjourned until nine O'clock until the morning," he said getting up and storming out of the courtroom.

Dale Forsyth felt elated as he left the courtroom. Things were going just like he wanted it to. The outbursts from the onlookers played directly into his hands. It was obvious that the people were in his corner, and impatient with Blunden. This was exactly what he wanted. It was critical for his argument because he knew that although he had a substantial amount of evidence, he was painfully aware that it was circumstantial. Apparently it was enough to convince the onlookers but not enough to convince a jury. Something really needed to be done in order to prove his case. He needed a smoking gun.

Early the next morning, the pretrial resumed with a standing room only crowd packed into the courtroom like sardines in a can.

The bailiff rapped his gavel several times and called the trial to order.

"Everyone rise."

Judge Terrance McGill entered the room and strode to his podium.

"This trial will now resume without any interruptions. Attorney Forsyth, continue your presentation."

"Your honor, I was saying that it makes no sense whatsoever, for the defendant to plead the Fifth Amendment to answer a simple question that has nothing to in criminate him, unless he's hiding something."

"I've thought about this since yesterday and am inclined to agree. Are there any objections from the defense?"

"No your honor" Blunden's replied.

"Then it's done. The defendant's plea is overruled. Mr. Spaulding will be required to answer the question."

Forsyth rose from his seat and took his time going to the podium.

"Thank you your honor. I'll repeat the question."

He turned and looked directly Spaulding.

"Where were you when you found the ruby?"

"Objection, your honor," shouted Blunden, "Mr. Spaulding is not on the witness stand."

"Objection overruled. Mr. Spaulding, answer the question."

Spaulding was visibly shaken, and obviously uncomfortable. He fidgeted nervously and spoke in a shaken voice.

"I was walking and jogging in a wooded area that I go to periodically."

"And where was this place?"

"Two or three miles outside of town"

"And while you were jogging, and or walking, you just so happened to stumble upon a ninety thousand dollar ruby just lying in the grass?"

"Yes"

"That's unbelievable. Why would such a thing just be lying in the grass in the middle of nowhere?"

"I don't know."

"Your honor, I would like for me and my colleague to approach the bench"

"Attorney Blunden, do you have objections to such a consultation?"

"No I don't your honor"

"Then both of you approach the bench."

Both Blunden and Forsyth approach the bench, and met with the judge in silence, and spoke in hushed tones not overheard by the courtroom. Forsyth requested a special hearing with the judge in his private chamber. Blunden offered no resistance.

When both attorneys returned to their seats, Judge McGill spoke.

"The court will recess for one hour" he said rising from his chair, and motioning to both attorneys to join him as he headed to his chambers.

At the announcement, the buzz and conversation in the courtroom began immediately. The bailiff informed the audience that the brief recess would give them the opportunity to visit the lounge for snacks and refreshments, but that no food or drinks would be allowed back in the courtroom.

When all three men were seated in the judge's chamber, judge McGill began.

"Dale, you asked to meet with me in private, and Mark had no objections, so I'll expect you to tell us what this is all about."

"Judge, first let me thank you for granting me my request. Spaulding's disclosure of where he found the ruby is significant for the prosecution as we believe it may offer us a clue as what he was trying to hide."

"Like what?" Blunden wanted to know.

"At this point we don't know, but it's obvious he is hiding something that he doesn't want us to know. During our investigation of Spaulding to this point, we have caught him in several lies and contradictions and see no reason not to believe that this is just another ploy by him. I think that even mark can agree that the preponderance of the evidence that we have amassed against him weighs heavily in our favor."

"What's your point?" the judge asked.

"We are requesting time for our investigator's to check out the area where Spaulding claims to have been walking or jogging in, to possibly pick up something that May help us solve this mystery."

"I agree too" Mark said. "I know how important this is to your case, Dale, which up to this point lacks real evidence against my client. Needless to say, I admit that I was a little surprised myself at the Fifth Amendment motion he made."

"How much time do you think you'll need?"

"A couple of weeks at least" Dale remarked.

"I can give you that much time," the judge said.

That was the news that Dale wanted to hear.

Just before they left the judge's chamber, he said that he would like to see the two attorneys shake hands. Both Dale and Mark shared a hearty laugh as they shook hands.

Upon reentering the courtroom, the bailiff called the meeting together, after the attorneys had both been seated.

"The court is now in order, the honorable judge Terrance McGill residing."

After calling the court in order, the judge made his statement.

"Me, and both attorneys have agreed to call a two week recess of this trial, in order to allow the prosecution adequate time to investigate the claim of the defendant, concerning the whereabouts of the ruby he claims to have found. Until then, the defendant will be released to go home, where he will be on house arrest, and be required to wear an ankle bracelet.This court is adjourned and will resume in two weeks" the judge ruled, and immediately left the courtroom.

At the announcement of the recess, mayhem broke out in the courtroom as reporters from every newspaper in town rushed from the room, and scurried to their papers in an attempt to be the first to break the news. The noise could be heard half a block away. People clambered to get out of the door first, many pushing and shoving.

Security took swift action to clear the doorway. Dale waited until the confusion died down, and then left the building to head to his office to notify all the necessary people he needed to talk to. Bob was at the trial and heard the judge's decision so there was no need to call him. He did, however, need to meet with Toby. He stopped him on the doorsteps of the court house and the two then immediately proceeded to go to Dale's office.

"Let's grab a cup of coffee, and talk about where we are and what needs to happen next."

Together they go inside where Dale tells his secretary to bring them coffee to his conference room.

Toby began by telling Dale what a great job he did at the hearing.

"I thought calling for the sidebar with the judge was an excellent idea."

"I'm glad that it worked out OK. The judge seemed to have tired of Spaulding's antics"

Toby agreed.

"I'm a little concerned, however, if two weeks will be enough time for your investigators to come up with something. If need be, I may be able to buy more time from the judge, but that's not guaranteed."

"Yeah, I know" muttered Toby. "We'll do our best."

"I know you will. I have all the confidence in the world with you and your agency. Still, there is the chance we may not be successful, and we'll have to let that rascal go."

"You can rest assured that won't happen" Toby said confidently. "I'll talk with James and John and round up my crew to begin to go to work. You're doing all that you can, and now we need to do the same."

Everywhere you that could think of, there was only one thing that occupied all of the residents of the town, talk of the pretrial. You heard it in the grocery stores, shopping Malls, Barber Shops, etc. you name it and it was there. People talked about in Taxi Cabs, city buses, train and bus stations. Families talked about it at the dinner tables in their houses, and in restaurants. When the recess was first announced, the telephones in Toby office, James and John's offices, Bob's office at police headquarters, all were literally jumping off the hooks.

Since the arrest of the thieves, and the recovery of the stolen jewels from Montero's, the public clamored for more action, not knowing all of the circumstances that were involved. Now instead of a grand jury trial of the criminals, there was a pretrial of a man believed to be a part of the thieves in custody, but had no real evidence against him, only circumstantial evidence. It was very confusing to the public. It was not obvious that all of the thieves had to be caught and tried before the case could be closed. Initially, there was no idea that another man was involved with the robbery, until the security guard at the jewelry store notified Toby and his agents of a possible get-a-way driver who was not identified and did not participate in the break in or the robbery.. Of course, with all of this under investigation the public had no idea of what was going on. Hopefully, the pretrial would fill in the blanks. James and John would certainly make certain that the newspapers got the whole story.

Over the next several days, as information about the pretrial were printed in newspapers, things had become clearer to the public, and the commotion and confusion began to wane. Reliford Investigations, which was one of James and John's subsidiaries, would now garner the lion share of the publicity. They made sure that as much information about the pre trail that could be revealed was. All eyes would now be on their private investigation agency. Of course, Toby relished the attention and the opportunity it afforded his new company. But at the same time, it made him a little nervous as well, because of all the pressure it put on them. He mentioned this to his team as he called them together to discuss their next move.

"We will really have to move fast," Toby began, "Because unless Bob can buy us more time with the judge, we only have two weeks to get the evidence that Dale, our attorney needs."

"What do we have to go on?" Jeremy asked.

"Not much," Toby replied. "According to Bob, there are several places outside of town that could be the place where Spaulding claims to have found the ruby."

"That's all that we have to go on?" Rod asked.

"That's it. I know it's not much, but it's all we have."

"Exactly how many places are there?" Jeremy wanted to know.

"Four."

"What are we supposed to be looking for.?" Dick asked.

"That's a good question" Toby replied. "What do all of you think?"

There were several minutes of silence as everyone wracked their brains for ideas. Finally, Ralph broke the silence.

"It would appear that we need to focus on why Spaulding was so reluctant to talk about where the place was that he found the ruby by trying to plead the fifth."

"To me that tells me that he didn't want to give away any clues that might help to give away its location."

"But why would that matter?"

"That's what we have to find out.'

"I have a hunch," Rod said. "It could be that it might tip off the place where the gang met after the robbery to split up the loot."

"That doesn't make a lot of sense. They could have done that just sitting in the car."

"That wouldn't work either. Nobody knew what each other had or how much. They would have wanted the booty to be shared equally."

They all agreed on that point by nodding their heads. Dick finally said something.

"If we don't have any idea of what to look for, it's not going to do much good just to look. The ruby has already been found, so what would be the purpose of just looking?"

"Dick's right," Toby said. "We have to come up with a reason or purpose for our search."

"Let me offer a suggestion," Dick said.

All of the investigators gave Dick their full attention as he was recognized as the only trained criminal investigator of the bunch.

"He could have been trying to hide the place where the gang met to divide the loot to everybody's satisfaction. Some kind of place or building to use since the crime had just been committed and the heat was on. They would need a place to hole up in."

"That's the best thing I've heard so far," Toby remarked. "At least that would give us a purpose for our searches and something to look for."

"So we need to search the four areas mentioned for a possible place where the thieves may have used to split the jewelry equally.

"Well, at least it gives us something." Rod acknowledged.

"We will need to search every nook and cranny of every location, leaving no stone unturned. It certainly makes it much better to have a sense of purpose in our searches, providing that what Dick has suggested is accurate." Toby said.

"If not, we're back to square one." Jeremy concluded.

"I want each area thoroughly covered from its beginning all the way to its ending in all directions. That's going to be a tall order, but it needs to be done, any other observations or comments?" Toby asked the group. When no one had any more to add, Toby goes to his chalk board.

"I'm going to divide the four areas into four groups, quadrants A,B,C and D." We'll begin with A, and I'll need a detailed report on each one when finished."

Quadrant A was a four mile wooded area outside of town with numerous trees and open grassland. The crew began to comb the area completely, leaving nothing overlooked. They searched for hours, often becoming agitated and impatient.

"This is for the birds," one complained.

"Yeah, I know," Dick said, "but it's all we've got."

It was close to nightfall when they finished and reported back to the investigation room.

"How'd it go?" Toby inquired "any luck?"

"Nothing, nothing at all!" one of them complained.

"We looked for everything," Rod said. "We looked for any signs of cigarette butts on the ground, the cigar wrappers that Spaulding smokes, tire tracks, discarded paper cups, empty whiskey flasks,

"Well, it's only the first day, so we'll try our hand again in the morning. One down and three to go," Toby noted. and anything else that would indicate the presence of people, there was not a thing."

"Are we overlooking anything?" Jeremy asked.

"Like what?" someone asked.

Nobody could think of anything.

The next day while his crew was out on another hunt, Bob called Toby from police headquarters.

"We need to meet .I have some important news to share with you."

"What about nine in the morning?" Toby suggested.

"Fine, see you then" Bob said.

Toby was beside himself as he sat in his chair puffing on his pipe. What could this possibly be about he wondered to himself? Bob never calls unless he has something significant or important to say or talk about. Was it something that he was doing wrong or had overlooked? Did someone have some legal issues involved with the case? He thought long and hard about these issues or possibilities, but came up with nothing. After a while he just settled back to enjoy his pipe and relax. He would know soon enough.

Later that afternoon the crew came back from their second day search. They were very tired and downtrodden.

"We looked overything over with a fine tuned comb, and found nothing. I've never seen so many trees, bushes and shrubbery to look under in my life. We didn't overlook anything," Jeremy lamented.

"I can back him up in that!" Ralph chimed in.

"I don't believe anybody has been in that spot in years," Rod claimed.

"At least all is not lost," Dick commented. "It is only day two of our investigation, and we do have another two days left, and at least we have an idea of what we're looking for maybe."

"we're all hoping that your hunch is correct, Dick, because without it I'm afraid we would sunk." On of them remarked.

"Yes, but it's the only thing that makes any sense.

"That's good thinking, Dick," Toby said." I know it's tedious and trying, but we have no other choice but to stay the course. Tomorrow we'll take the third quadrant. Right now, let's all get a nice big cup of coffe, because I have something to talk with all of you about."

He buzzed his secretary on the intercom and told her to bring them all coffee and a few doughnuts.

"I know that all of you are tired and hungry and want to get home, you've been gone practically the whole day. I got a call from Bob at headquarters a while ago, and he wants to meet with us tomorrow. I have no idea what it's about, but you know Bob, he never calls unless it's important information to share with us."

"Wow! I can't wait to hear what that that will be all about," said Rod, suddenly reinvigorated."

Me too," chimed in several others.

The secretary brought in the coffee requested, and they all sat back and relaxed. Toby relit his pipe and observed the boy's faces and body language as they fixed their coffee to their liking. He was not worried, but just a little nervous, because they didn't have a lot of time left, and so far it looked as though they were looking for a needle in a haystack.

It sort of reminded him of the sinking feeling he had back in Midway when he was involved in searching for clues to get Rod and Jeremy set free. Eventhough they were exhausted and worn, Toby knew that because they were all young men, they were resilient and strong and would bounce back quickly.

"Why are we so despondent?" asked Jeremy. "We haven't had anything to do since our undercover operation, and now that we have been assigned with probably the most critical task in this whole thing, we sit around complaining.. Come on, let's pick it up."

"I agree," added Ralph.

"Fellas, it's only natural to feel a little down in the dumps at a time like this. I was just thinking as I watched all of you just a second ago, of how much you reminded me of myself doing work to get two of you free in Midway. There's nothing out of the ordinary that you're going through" Toby told them.

"You guys have done a tremendous job with everything so far, and I know you will do the same this time. It's not your fault that you have nothing to go on but a hunch

They spent the rest of their time in the office encouraging each other after Toby's words. When they all left to go home shortly afterwards, they felt much better. Toby drove home feeling a little ambivalent himself. Pulling into his driveway, he was quickly snapped back to his old self when he smelled the aroma of Peg's cooking.

"You look like you could use a good meal," she told him as he sat down at the dinner table.

He nooded his head in agreement, and gave her a nice smile of appreciation.

"You've lways known whenever I need a little spark or uplifting," he told her, as he dove into his meal of steak, mashed potatoes and green beans. He hadn't realized he was so hungry.

"The desert that I have for you will also help you feel much better."

"What's that?" he asked.

"You'll find out soon enough," she answered with a wink.

He smiled knowingly as he finished his dinner.

At nine the next morning in his office, he met with Bob and his crew to have the discussion that Bob talked about over the phone.

"I got a report yesterday from the FBI in answer to my request, about another robbery of precious jewels somewhere else in the world, that involved the theft of rubies among other things. They told me that about a month ago there was a giganic robbery in Cairo, Egypt involving diamonds and precious gems from a diamond cutter, that included the theft of a huge Heirloom ruby. I think that our ruby may be a small part of the original stone, that was valued at several million dollars."

"What makes you think that?" Toby asked.

"The report of the gemologist about the ruby that Spaulding gave to his mother, and what it was worth. And the fact that he said it was obvious just a piece of a larger one."

Everyone present was stunned and said nothing for a moment while the information sunk in.

"Yes, that's exactly the way I felt when they told me."

"What do you think your next plan of action will be with this information?" Toby asked him.

"I don't know exactly," he responded, "Except that eventually it will turned over to the authorities in Cairo to be returned to it's rightful owner after it's been investigated."

"When do you think that might take place?" Dick wanted to know.

"It can't be until after the trial of the thieves take place, and sentencing has been done."

"Another mystery surrounding this ruby," exclaimed Rod, "I've never seen anything it."

"Me either," Jeremy agreed.

"Where do you think this leaves us?" Jeremy asked Bob.

"Stuck in the middle I'm afraid. You've uncovered the ruby, but now it must remain in the hands of the police until we take action."

"What about poor Mr. Smith at Montero's, whos'e wxpecting to get his ruby returned after the trial is over?" Rod asked.

"Toby, we will have to leave that up to you to explain the circumstances." Bob answered.

"Wow! this has certainly thrown a monkey wrench in everything." Ralph noted.

"You can say that again," Dick agreed.

"My plan is to have Toby and Dick travel to Cairo after the trial is over, and turn the ruby over to the proper authorities there." He finished. "Of course, we will need to get James and John's approval to use Toby. So you can see just how important the work that all of you are doing right now.we first need to get this pre trial invoving Spaulding over with in order for us to preceed."

This perked up the enthusiasm and energy of all of the investigators immediately. Toby recognized it right away. The very first thing that he planned to do was to have a good talk with Smith.

After the meeting with Bob was over, Toby and his crew took a while to go over the information just handed them.

"Well, what do you think guys?"

"This makes us feel important again" one of them noted.

"I know that this latest development will floor James and John."

"I'll call them as soon as this meeting is over."

Everyone agreed, and had no additional questions or observations.

Toby then called the corporate office that afternoon. James answered the phone.

"Good to hear from you, Toby." He said, "How's everything going, John is in a meeting with a new prospective client?"

"Everything is going OK. I was calling to tell you about the latest development here. I was just notified by Bob at headquarters that the ruby we have just recovered is part of a large jewelry robbery that took place in Cairo about a month ago."

"My goodness. This gets more interesting all the time."

"Yes indeed," Toby said," and that's not the half of it. They want to turn it over to the authorities there, so that it can be returned to its rightful owner, and also be used in their own investigation."

"When do they want to do this.?"

"As soon as the grand jury tries and convicts the criminals who robbed Moneros, once we finish with the pre trial of Hank Spaulding."

"Oh Yes, by the way how's that investigation going?"

"At rhis point not too good. So far we haven't been able to come up with anything. The crew has been working hard scouring the cites that might have been used by the thieves right after the heist, in order to connect Spaulding to them."

"The whole town is anxiously waiting for that to happen."

"The crew will be going out tomorrow to search the third of four cites.Time is winding down and we're beginning to feel the pressure a little."

"What will you do if time runs out on you?"

"Well, we may possibly have one out. Bob in confident that the judge is sympathetic to our efforts, and he may be able to buy us a lttle more time if that happens, but I don't think that it will be for long if he does, but we can't count on that."

"We'll keep our fingers crossed for you. Is there anything else that we can do?"James asked.

"Yes there is by the way. A couple of things actually. First Bob does not want anything to be mentioned about the ruby being returned to Cairo."

"Gotcha" James responded.

"Secondly, he wants me to get permission from you to accompany, Dick Wingate to Cairo when he goes to return the ruby because it's too expensive for him to travel with it alone."

"That makes a ton of sense. I'll get with John about everything when we talk, but I'm certain that there won't be any problem letting you go to Cairo.There won't be any mention about the ruby going there either."

"Good," Toby responded. "I'll make sure that we keep you abreast of everything."

"I know you will. It was nice to talk with you. Call anytime if need be" he told Toby.

After their conversation ended, Toby lit his pipe and contemplated his next move, which as a conversation with Smith to bring him up to date on everything. Toby's crew headed out again that morning and Toby then called Smith;s office.

"Gary, Toby here" he said, "we need to meet and talk about what's going on now."

"Toby, it's good to hear from you. I've ben following everything in the newspapers."

"What I want to talk with you about has nothing to do with what's been printed and talked about. When is a good time for us to talk"

"Any time is a good time for me, you know that," Smith responded.

"How about noon this afternoon.?"

"Sounds like a plan. See you then."

Toby was invited by Smith to sit down and have a cup of coffee with him. Toby agreed and then started to begin a conversation with Smith with a serious and grim look on his face.

"I can tell by your appearance that this is not going to be good news," Smith said.

"Well, not really bad news in a sense," Toby began. "it's about the ruby of course which you know that the police is holding."

Smith nodded his acknowledgement.

"I doubt if you'll ever get it back."

"Oh wow! Why? What do you mean by that?" Smith inqired.

"The police recently received news from the FBI that your ruby is probably connected to a jewelry heist that took place in Cairo, Egypt about a month ago. Our gemologist here in the bronx has certified that your ruby was carved from a much larger stone earlier."

A look of disbelief etched visibly on the face of Smith as he listened to what Toby was telling him. He was completely dumbfounded and speechless. Toby noted his response and was completely sympatheic for him. They both took deep gulps of coffee, and just sat sat looking at each other for a moment.

"This comes as a surprise," Smith finally said, "but not as a total shock. I suspected something was going to happen when I received word about the true value of my ruby.What do they intend to do with it?"

"Once the grand Jury triial is over, the ruby is planned to be returned to Egypt in an attempt to get it to its rightful owner."

"That means that for me, I'll not only be without the ruby for my aniversary, but out twenty thousand dollars as well."

"I'm sorry about that. I'll talk to the police and see if there is any way possible to at least get your money returned to you."

"Any thing at all that you can do will be extremely appreciated, he responded. "I've been kicking myself every day for being so stupid and gullible, allowing such an idiotic thing like that to happen in the first place."

"Don't feel like that. All of us has been taken for a ride like that at one time or another. But it does serve to remind us to be more careful with those we do business with or think we can trust. How's business going otherwise?"

"We're doing OK. Sales are continuing on as usual and we're still planning on our thirty fifth anniversary celebration with or without the ruby."

"That's good," Toby remarked.

After their meeting was over, Toby headed back to his office. He was glad that the meeting with Gary was over.Now he sat back to light his pipe while waiting for a client that he had scheduled to arrive this afternoon, before his meeting with Smith. As he was waiting, his phone rang. It was Bob from headquarters.

"How'd the meeting with Smith go?" he asked.

"About what you'd expect. He was shocked of course, about the news of his ruby."

"I imagined he would be," Bob replied.

"What's up?" Toby asked.

"I just received word from our attorney, that Spaulding agreed to take a lie detector test, which he had previously refused to take before."

"What happened?"

"He passed it. He is still claiming that he did not steal the ruby that he gave to his dying mother. He's up to something, I just don't know exactly what."

"What does this mean?" Toby asked.

"Even if the judge orders Spaulding to stand trial with the others, we still have to prove that he stole the ruby somehow."

"Why is that important?" Toby asked.

"Even though he's suspected of being part of the criminals, it still has yet to be proven. the mystery of how he came to be in possesion of the ruby still needs to be answered. By maintaining his plea of not being involoved in the robbery itself, still leaves us to prove our point. We've arrested him simply because he had the ruby, which the others claim to know nothing about."

"But what good will that do him?" Toby wanted to know.

"A great deal. he's is still trying to get off scott free. His lawyer has probably told him to maintain his plea, because up to now we still have no definitive proof of anything. Our claim that he was the get-a-way driver is only circumstantial as far as they are concerned."

"But how can they do that? He was arrested because he had the stolen ruby."

"I know, but that still does not prove that he couldn't have found it innocently. We arrested him only because he had stolen contraband on his person."

"Man, this just doesn't make any sense! we found his cigar butts in the alley behind the jewelry store where his car was spotted at the time of the robbery, and also later in his car. he gave the stolen ruby to his dying mother, which we also found on him later at his house, and this is not enough?"

"This only points out how difficult it is to prosecute the Alfred Plea. The problem is that he was never identified by an eye witness at any point, not even by the thieves themselves, and his attorney knew this. So now you can see just how important the search is that you're doing."

"I see it now," Toby admitted.

"It's like trying to solve a murder without the murder weapon or a body." Bob explained.

"So what's his plan?"

"I wish I knew. I know he and his lawyer are up to something though."

"Anyway, it was good talking to you," Toby told him.

"Let me know if your crew comes up with anything," Bob said before the two hung up.

Toby was very troubled by the conversation with Bob. He lit his pipe and tried to relax himself but with little success. Everything now hinged upon his crew. There was literally nothing else left. He felt powerless.

Later that evening his crew returned, again empty handed, tired and dejected. Toby told them about his conversation with Bob earlier.

"I just don't understand how small technicalities could pave the way for somebody like Spaulding to have a chance to walk." Jeremy griped.

"I know it's frustrating but everything must be proven **beyond the shadow of a doubt**." Toby reminded them.

"So everything that we have done literally amounts to nothing." Rod lamented.

"Not exactly. We have provided our attorney with a bevy of evidence that clearly points the finger at Spaulding. It was enough to convince the judge to give us time to investigate Spaulding's attempt at a cover up. So it has had some positive impact."

Getting back to the business of the third day of searching, Toby was very interested in hearing what his crew had to say as he observed their body language.

"We looked everywhere," Jeremy said, "under every rock, behind every tree and under every bush. Nothing."

"All this because of one little lie that sucker has told," Rod said angrily.

"I can certainly understand where you're coming from," agreed Ralph.

"Stop and think for a minute," Toby interjected. "if you were on trial would'nt you want to be proven innocent beyond any reasonable doubt?"

"Well, when you put it that way, of course." Jeremy conceded.

"I know it looks bleak," Toby acknowledged, but there's always tomorrow. go home, relax and get some sleep. We have a mighty big day coming up."

Toby went home after the meeting, but discovered that he was unable yo do what he had suggested to the others earlier. He could'nt go to sleep no matter how much he tried. He had not experienced a night like this since he fretted over a sense of powerless in the boy's trial in Midway over a year ago.

The next day, things started out as usual. The boys met that morning and received their final instructions from Toby.

"I know this is the final day of our investigation, but I'm still hopeful that something will turn up. Just go out and do the best you can."

Toby phoned their attorney Dale when the crew had gone out the door.

"Well the guys have has just left, and they came up with nothing again yesterday. This is our last day to find something. Do we have any other options left"

"I'm going to talk to judge McGill today and see if he is willing to grant us a little more time. I know that will be very difficult for him to do, seeing all of the publicity and excitement that this pre trial has generated, but it's all we have left. Let me get on it right away."

"Thanks Dale," Toby said. "If there's any one person that we can depend on, it's you. You have been tremendous so far. You're every bit as good your reputation says you are."

"Well, hold your applause," Dale tells Toby, "we are'nt through yet."

"That's just my way of saying thanks for everything. James and John certainly knew what they were doing when they recommended you to us."

"Well thanks for the complement. I'll call judge McGill now."

After his conversation with Toby, Dale called the judge's office. His secretrary answered the phone.

"Judge McGill's office," a soft sultry voice answered.

"This is attorney Dale Forsyh."

"Oh yes, Mr. Forsyth. The judge will be glad to hear from you. right now, however, he's in court. I'll have him call you as soon as he finishes."

"Thank you" Dale replied.

Back in Toby's office, he has John on the line.

"This is our last day of the investigation, and so far the boys have come up with nothing. Dale is working with judge Mc Gill to try and buy us more time if we need it."

"That sounds pretty bleak," John said. "as long as Dale is on the job, I'll remain a little optimistic."

"He's a fantastic attorney, John."

"I know. He's worked with me and james on several occasions; trust issues, law suits, mergers, you name it, he's been the man."

"I'll call you just as soon as I hear back from him."

"Fine, I'll be waiting. Good luck with everything. Goodbye."

Toby enjoyed smoking his pipe as usual, when another client that he was expecting at any time was announced by his secretary.

"Come on in, Brad, have a seat" Toby said to the man that had hired him to find a person involved in a hit and run accident involving his mini van.

Folowing his meeting with the man, Toby was entrenched deep in thought when his phone. It was Dick.

"Toby, I've got good news for a change. The guys have found an old abandoned hunting lodge in the woods here."

"Jeez –o-petes!" Toby blurted out, having absolutely no idea what the phrase meant. "It looks like you might have been right, Dick."

"Well, I certanly hope so. It's the only thing that we have found so far, and the last cite on our agenda. there's nothing else out here period."

"This is awesome! Tell the guys to head back here to the office, while I call your boss at headquarters and give him the news."

Toby was delirious with excitement. He sat there too stunned to move for several seconds. He had Bob on the phone without realizing that he had dialed him.

"Bob, you need to sit down."

"Toby, what's up?"

"It looks as though your investigator was right. **They found the shack that Dick suggested would be somewhere.**" Toby managed to say.

"Let's try not get too excited yet. All they found was an abanded shack that might be something or not something. I'm trying not to get too excited until we've have a chance to check it out. I'll have my entire forensic team to go and give the place a thorogh going over, from top to bottom, and front and back. They'll dust the place for evertyhing. If there's anything to be found, they'll find it. I guarantee. Give me the location of the place."

Toby laid the phone down on his desk, and went to get the paper that the directions of all four cites were written on. As soon as he found it, he picked up the phone and gave the directions of the place to Bob.

"We're on it as of yesterday," Bob said.

Toby waited about an hour or so for his crew to arrive, then he heard the rushing of feet and the anxious voices of his investgators as they came through thr door. He was excited to hear and see the enthusiasm from them, it was quite refreshing for a change. He was already smoking his pipe and relaxed in his chair.

"We stayed until the forensic squad arrived and they roped off the area" Dick chimed.

"What a great experience," clamored Jeremy, his face beaming.

"Just when it seemed that all was lost, we finally struck pay dirt," Rod exclaimed.

"You'd never know what a relief it was to finally see something come of all the work we did!" he said with gusto.

"I've never seen so much forensic equipment unloaded in my life" marveled Ralph.

Toby sat back relishing the moment. He felt so good for all of them. They had worked so hard but never gave up, eventhough they were tried to the very upmost at times. They had covered numerous miles of woodland, shrubbery, bushes and land filled with hundreds of trees to no avail until today. He let them express their exuberance and excitement over cups of coffee and doughnuts prepared for them by his secretary.

When they all seemed to have calmed down a little, Toby beganto talk to them.

"This is indeed a great triumph for us, no doubt," he began, "but let's not forget, nothing has been decided about anything yet! All we know is that a shack has been found and nothing else."

"But it does appear that what Dick had speculated about, could very well have been accurate" Rod said.

"That very well could be true," Toby acknowledged, "but we have to wait until the police report is completed before we breathe a word of this to anyone, and I mean to no one."

Toby's caution seemed to diminish some of the enthusiasm in his crew, which of course was the aim of his discourse. Be that as it may, he was very excited and euphoric himself, but found it necessary to curb his excitement as an example before the crew. They discussed the events of the day while in the meeting, and then left to go home and back to work.

Toby sat on pins and needles for hours until he received a phone call from Bob.

"Toby, Bob here. "I will call you sometime tomorrow with the results of our lab work, to tell you what we found. I know how anxious you are to know something, and so am . I'l call attorney Forsyth and let him know that he doesn't have to bother the judge about giving us more time."

"That's music to my ears," Toby remarked.

"Don't say anything about this, especially to James and John," Bob said.

"I know, I've already told my crew the exact same thing."

Tomorrow couldn't come soon enough Toby thought to himelf, as he settled back in his chair to enjoy the peace and quiet of a soothing and settled mind. This was the most peaceful feeling that he had felt in weeks.

Bob called Toby the next day as he sat waiting in his office smoking his pipe.

"I've got some good news for you," he began. Toby instantly sat up and was all ears.

"We found the fingerprints of all the prisoners, including those of Spaulding all over the building. They left the paper cups they used to finish off a fifth of whiskey, and cigarette butts galore, including the cigar butts smoked by Spaulding. We matched all of it with their DNA samples here at the station.

"So this means that we have finally nailed Spaulding after all."

"Yes, but it only proved that he was with them in the shack, but not that he is guilty of stealing the ruby, or that he was actually the get-a-way driver."

"But it does prove that he was a member of the gang, or at least knows them since they were all locked up together a while ago."

"It does. The noose is certanly tightening around his neck. I'll bet my bottom dollar, though, that he will still maintain his plea of innocense about how he came in possession of the ruby."

"To what avail"" Toby wanted to know.

"I don't know what he has up his sleeve, but I bet Dale will find out."

"So now he can be tried with the rest of them in court."

"Maybe, once the judge bounds him over to the grand jury after receiving this information."

"Just like heavy weight champion Joe lewis said when he fought light heavy champion Billy Conn, 'you can run but you can't hide'"

"I think that's appropriate here"Bob agreed."I'll keep you posted."

Toby took this time now to bring James and John up to date on everything that had transpired.

"Now that's what you call cutting it close. Too close for my comfort," James said.

"That goes for me as well," ageed John.

"I hope that we can now finally bring this fiasco to a close,Toby mused.

"I think that goes for all of us, they both agreed.

The pre trial resumed again two days later, which was within the time that the judge had granted the prosecution its two week recess.

Needless to say, you couldn't squeeze a sardine into the courtroom. Ralph noticed as he scanned over the room that Brenda, Hanks sister was present seated by herself. He walked over to her and sat down beside her. He had almost forgotten how attrative she was for a woman her age.

"How have you been?" he asked her.

"OK., I'm managing."

"I'm sorry that you have to go through with this so soon after your mother's death."

"That's alright. I"ll survive."

"I'd like for you meet a few people before you leave to go back home when we finish here."

"OK."

The bailiff's rap of a gavel got everyone's immediate attention.

"All rise,"the bailiff said. "The court is now in seesion, the honorable judge Terrance McGill, presiding."

After the judge was seated,the trial resumed.

"Is the prosecution and the defense present to begin?"

Both parties stood up and nodded.

"Is the defendant present?"

Spaulding stood up and nodded. Ralph noted the look of exasperation on Brenda's face. Afterall, this was her brother.

"Then let us begin. Attorney Forsyth, you may continue."

A hush fell over the room. You could only hear the air conditioning unit humming.

"The prosecution calls Mr. Hank Spaulding to the witness chair."

Hank stood up, a little surprised, but apparently not visibly troubled as he took his seat.

"Mr. Spaulding, what were you doing at the old ababdoned hunting lodge on the outskirts of town?"

"What time are you talking about? I go there from time to time while hunting."

"Hunting for what? Deer season is over."

"Sometimes I hunt for squirrels, rabbits, ground hogs, and things like that."

"Do you remember when was the last time that you were there?"

"Maybe two, three weeks ago."

"Are you sure that was the last time you were there? be careful, you're under oath."

"Yes, I think so."

"then why were your fingerprints lifted there, by the police only two days ago?"

A murmur was heard in the courtoom.

"What do you mean?"

"Two days ago, the investigators at the Reliford private detective agency, informed the police that that they had found a shack in the woods on the outskirts of town, that they believed was used by the thieves just after robbing Monsero's jewelry store as a hideout. DNA testing proved that the identity of all the thieves were all confirmed."

"Objection, your honor. That's just speculation. The prosecution is badgering and leading the witness!" Blunden shouted.

"Objection overruled. Mr. Spaulding answer the question."

"I have no idea how my fingerprints were found there two days ago."

"The police report says that all of the prints found there were taken at the same time, including yours"

"That's a lie" shouted Spaulding, standing up on his feet, his face a bright red, his brow glistening with perspiration, and his hands now trembling. Disorder erupted in the courtroom, and the judge banged his gavel on his desk.

"Mr. Spaulding, sit down! Another outburst like that and I'l have you removed and held in contempt." Spaulding immediately sat down. He suddenly felt trapped and desparate.

"All of the evidence was confirmed as being left at the Same time by the police's DNA testing. I rest my case your honor" Dale concluded as he strode confidently back to his seat.

Judge Terrance McGill waited until all the commotion had died down, to render his decision.

"In light of all the evidence rendered thus far in this courtroom, I find it necessary to remand the defendant, Hank Spaulding, to be bound over to a grand jury for further investigation. However, until then, he will remain on house arrest and be required to continue wearing an ankle bracelet. A trial date will be set later, and jury selection will begin then."

All hell broke loose, and judge McGill was ushered to safety by security. This is exactly what the entire city had been waiting for! Finally, the resolution of this case was finally drawing to a conclusion, with the arrest and trial of all parties involved. All that was left now, was for everyone to await the outcome.

Toby and Bob met immediately after the trial with Dale in the court's hearing room.

"You did it again," Bob told Dale, giving him a firm handshake and a hug, his face beaming."When everything began to look bleak just a few days ago, I told Toby that as long as you were on the case, that you would pull us through."

"He sure did," Toby exclaimed, also giving him a handshake and a hug. "You were brilliant. It was great to see you at work. You were everything that Bob said you were."

As they were wrapping up their meeting, Ralph came in the room to introduce them to Brenda.

"Gentlemen, I want all of you to meet Brenda Spaulding, Hank's sister. It was she that gave me the information about the ruby given to her mother by Hank, and permission to retrieve it when her mother had passed. She also callled me when her brother picked up the ruby. I don't know what I would have done without her."

Dale spoke to her first to let her know that the judge will have to set a date for the grand jury trial.

"I know that it will difficult for you to have to sit through the proceedings."

"Only because he's my brother. If he's found to be guilty, he deserves to be pinished along with the rest of them."

"She's quite a remarkable woman." Toby said to Ralph. "You were right about her."

After the meeting was over, Ralph walked Brenda to her car.

"Oh, by the way," she told Ralph, "Tony Robinson the diamond expert that examined mother's ruby, has been calling me to go out with him. You know he's single, and has been divorced for over twenty years."

"That doesn't surprise me in the least. Just look at you. what single man wouldn't want to take you out."

"Your'e kind."

"No, just truthful."

Toby called togather his crew to the office, to discuss the findings of the legal proceedings thus far.

"We still have ways to go before this is over. His maintaining his inncence about simply finding the ruby, could possibly mean that he could walk away, or at worse receive a much less significant sentece than the others, and I personally don't want to see that happen."

"But just being by only the **suspected** get-a-way driver, he is nevertheless a part of the theft anyway by being an accomplice. he's guilty by association." Dick reasoned.

"That's true," Toby agreed, "but if successful, he could get off with a lot less severe punishment than the others. That appears to be his goal, and I for one, am not willing to let him get away with that."

"He did appear to be bellerant and defiant," noted Rod.

"Unfortunately, we have to wait until the jury trial, and then depend on Dale again to do his usual astounding work."

"I believe the deck is still stacked in our favor" Rod said.

"I agree," Toby said.

The meeting adjourned and the investigators were dismissed.

"I'll call you when I need you" Toby told them as they left the premise.

Two days later, Toby's telephone rang as he sat puffing on his pipe and enjoying a rare time of peace and quiet. It was Ralph.

Toby, I'm just callng to inform you that Beth has just been taken to the hospital to have her baby."

"I'm not sure that I heard correctly. Did you say that Beth was on her way to the hospital to have her baby."

"That's right. The ambulance is on the way as we speak."

"I'll let the other guys know, and we'll meet at the hospial. Congratulations, Jeremy, "This is certainly unepected great news."

"I was so nervous that I couldn't drive myself, but I did call an ambulance."

"You did good," Toby told him. "See you at the hospital."

Toby immediately called his group together and gave them the news. They immediately piled into their vehicles and headed for the hospital.

"well, Jeremy is finally going to be a father,"

After going to the waiting room, where all of the expected fathers gathered to await the news of their wive's delivery, the crew with the exception of Toby and Rod, were on pins and needles. This was their first experience with such a thing. Soon Jeremy entered the room escorted by a nurse from the operating room.

"Mr. Mc Cutchin has chosen not to go to the operating room for his wife's delivery. We will come back out immediately following the delivery to give you all the results."

"That's the same decision that I made myself," Toby volunteered.

"Me too," chimed in Rod.

"I was OK., until they wanted me to put on a gown, a cap, and gloves, before going into the operating room. That was all too traumatic for me."

"Yes, I know the feeling," Rod said.

After what seemed like an eternity, they witnessed the nurses coming into the room announcing the birth of each waiting father, who all laughed, shook hands and congratulated each other by lighting up a cigar in celebration. One of the men said that he had waitied for over eight hours to receive the news.

"Well, I guess it's now time for me to pay my dues," Jeremy said, as he observed the other men in the room.

After what seemed like forever, a nurse came in and announced the birth of jeremy's baby.

"Congratulations. Mr. Cutchin, you are the proud father of a baby boy."

All of the guys erupted into cheers and handshakes.

"Can I see my wife now?" Jeremy asked her immediately.

"Yes. Follow me," the nurse told him.

Jeremy was all too eager to obey. When he left the room, Toby and the guys all lit up their cigars which he had provided. When Jeremy entered the delivery room, Beth had the baby cradled in her arms and stroking his medium brown hair with a glowing demeanor.

"Isn't he just precious?" she beamed.

"He sure is," Jeremy exclaimed, sticking out his chest. "A chip off the old block."

He was the spitting image of Jeremy, but fortunately inherited Beth's looks.

"How much did he weigh?" Jerey asked.

"Eight and a half pounds."

"Was the delivery very difficult?"

"I would imagine so. They gave me a spinal epidural for pain, so I can't be moved for several hours. They'll come and let you know what room I'll be in."

"All of the guys are here, and they're anxious to see you and the baby."

"That's nice. I'm a liottle groggy from the medication, so I think I'll take a nap now."

"That's a good idea. We'll all be here when you wake up."

After beth dozed off, Jeremy went back out to the waiting room completely on another planet. **He was now a father!** When he burst into the room, one of the guys immediatedly shoved a cigar in his mouth, and slapping him all over his back. Toby just sat smiling. These were his boys. They celebrated for over two hours, until the nurse poked her head in the door and told them what room Beth was in.

They proceeded quietly down the hospital corridor to Beth's room. She was now half awake, and gave them all a weak wave of her hand They told her that they weren't staying long, because they wanted her to rest. The nurse in the room informed them that when they were ready, she would take them to the newborn nursery room to see the baby.

"You'll have to stay outside of the nursery, and look in the window for baby McCuthcin."

When they arrived at the newborn nursery unit, jeremy immediately pressed his nose against the glass.

"There he is over by the water container," he said pointing.

They all focused their eyes on the little tot, laying quietly on his back. He had a head full of thick hair, and was only one of two newborns, that lay still in their cribs. Toby told them to observe how each baby's temperament and dispositions were already evident. Some of the babies were crying so hard that their little faces were beet red, and their legs kicking.

"Just look at little Jeremy, already calm and cool like his ol' man." Rod said, slapping jeremy on his back. They all laughed together.

"We'd all better be going," Toby said. "I know that Jeremy is going to stay overnight with Beth, and sleep on the cot provided for him in the room. Give beth our regards," he concluded.

"I will fellas, and thanks again for coming."

Early the next morning, beth and Jeremy were busy on the telephone. First Beth called her mother back in Midway.

"Mom, this is Beth," she said when her mother answered.

"Oh baby, it's so good to hear from you. How are you?"

"I'm fine. I'm calling you from the hospital."

"What! Why are you calling from a hospital? What's wrong?"

"I'm fine grandma."

"Who's grandma? Beth what in the world are you talking about?"

"I just had my baby last night, an eight and a half pound boy. I'm sorry for not keeping you up to date about my pregnancy. I know you were not thilled when I married jeremy and moved to New York."

"I got over that a while ago. How's he doing?"

"He's fine. He's so proud of being a brand new father."

"I really am a real live grandmother! Congratulations, baby." Mrs. McCallister exclaimed loudly.

"We haven't named him yet, but his middle name will be Toby."

"How is Toby and the agency by the way?"

"They're all doing great."

"I still regret the way that I treated him when he tried to help us when your brother hit you."

"That's OK mom.

"When will I be able to see my grandson?"

"The guys are in the middle of a trial right now, prosecuting a bunch of thieves who robbed a jewelry store here about a month ago. When the trial is over, me and Jeremy will come to Midway to see you, and visit everybody."

"That'll be great. Wait until I spread the news about my grandson." She beamed.

When Beth finished her conversation with her mother, Jeremy immediately took the phone and called his dad.

"Dad, this is Jeremy" he said when his father answered.

"I didn't call you last night, because I didn't want to alarm you and mom before anything happened. But me and beth had our baby last night, an eight pound baby boy." Jeremy said proudly

"**Yeah**!" shouted his father." For heaven's sake boy, you should have called us anyway. Congratulations are in order. I guess you think you're grown now," his father teased him.

They both had a hearty laugh together.

"Here's your mom" John told him.

"Son, I heard you talking to your father about the baby. I'm so happy I just don't know what to say. Congratulations to you and Beth. I know she was just happy to see ten fingers and ten toes! That's one of the first things that mothers look for when their babies are born."

"We'll be up to see our grandson this afternoon. He will have the biggest baby shower that you can imagine." John told his son. "Just wait until James hears the news."

Jeremy heard the whoops and yells of his parents before the phone completely hung up. He and beth just hugged each other tightly, savoring the time together. They were truly as one flesh, just like the Bible said. After making their calls and spending time together, they both went to the newborn nursery to see their baby. Beth had decided that she would breast feed, and did so while they visited together.

Jeremy's mind went back to the time in Midway a little over a year ago, as Beth breast fed the baby. He thought about the events right after the trial of him and Rod, being tried for vehicular homicide after being framed by the town coroner, to coverup for his son who actually did the hit and run. That was when he and Beth fell hopelessly in love.

Because he was an outsider from up north, and traveling with Rod who was black, both stuck in this small rural souuthern town of 740 people, they were already guilty in the couurt of public opinion.Toby, the sheriff at the time, investigating their case, was the only one who belived in their innocence, other than Beth. As they were locked up while the trial was going on, Beth visited him in the jail every day, often bringing him and Rod refreshments.

When he was discouraged or downtrodden by the events taking place, she would console him and perk him up. Toby allowed her to come and go at will, while the town's people criticized her for supporting the two outsiders. Some of them wanted her fired from the job she held at the town grocery store. She was called a 'nigger lover' because Rod was a companion with Jeremy. Still she perservered.

When the trial was over, and they were found innocent of the charges, he told her mother that he wanted to marry her after he went back to New York school for his graduation. She balked and had no comment whatsoever. He later found out that she was not happy with the thought of her daughter moving away.

Still, when he went back to Midway following his graduation to get her, her mother still reluctant, nevertheless, let her go. When they arrived back at home together,his father, John, and his partner James, Rod's dad, both gave them a wedding to remember. It seemed as though the entire city of the bronx showed up.

When Beth finished breast feeding the baby, he started to cry. This interrupted his thoughts and jolted him back to the present. After giving her time to gather herself, he remembered that the baby still did not have a name. He had several possible names rambling through his head, but was unable to to decide on one.

"What do you think we ought to name him?" he asked Beth.

"I don't know" Beth responded. "What do you think about Terrence?"

"Terrence McCutchin … it has a nice ring to it. Don't you think?" he asked Beth.

"Yes, I like it."

"Then Terence it is."

Since the time that Ralph and Karen first met over four months ago, during the time the undercover work was being done, the two have become inseperable. With every waking moment that was available

to them when Ralph wasn't working, or Karen not in school, they spent together. They were hopelessly in love and struggling mightily to control their sexual urges for one another. On numerous occasions, Ralph went home suffering from a severe case of blue balls, that happens when a man becomes extremely sexaully aroused, but does not have sex to relieve the pressure. The pain is excruciating.

Whenever that happened, Karen truly felt sorry for him, but Ralph refused to blame her, because he was as much to blame as she was. It had reached the point where something significant had to be done. They struggled with the moral issue of having sex outside of wedlock, especially if it was considered to be just recreational, as both were deeply religious, and wanted to do the right thing according to their beliefs.

"I just can't go on like this," Ralph complianed. Karen expressed the same sentiment.

"I guess the only solution is to get married" Ralph said.

"You make it sound like a death sentence or something." Karen lamented.

"I'm very sorry if I did. That's the furthest thing from what I meant."

"I know that," Karen confessed. "But can you see what this is doing to us.?"

"I think we need to get married very soon. Are you ready to be my wife, Karen?"

"I believe I was ready for that from the beginning."

"Then will you marry me?"

"Yes. I want you to meet my mother so we can tell her of our decision."

"What if she doesn't like me?"

"Don't be silly. She'll love you just as I do."

"Now that we're officially engaged to be married, and our intentions are honest, I want to make love to you right now."

Karen offered no resistance to Ralph's advances. They kissed each other deeply and passionately, literally sucking the life out of each other. Karen moaned softly as Ralph laid her on her down on the couch, and began to unbutten her blouse, exposing her ample breasts, full, succulent and firm, with no bra.

"Ralph, You need to know that I'm a virgin." She moaned in a voice filled with desire, and feeling his raging manhood straining to escape the confines of his pants.

That stopped him in his tracks. He was shocked to find a woman her age that was still a virgin.

"Are you kidding me?"

"Not about something as serious as this. Like I told you before, my mother wanted me to absorb myself in my shool work, and not get involved in these kind of situations. She taught me how to satisfy myself when I felt urges like this. You are the very first man that I have allowed myself to have these kinds of feelings about."

Ralph felt like he had struck gold. He would not let anything spoil this.

"Introduce me to your mother tomorrow," he said seriously.

"OK."

The next day was Saturday, and so there was no reason for them not to make it happen. Karen called her mother, and she agreed to meet with them without knowing what the purpose was for. The all met that afternoon, and Karen's mother had prepared a lunch for them. Ralph noticed right away what a fine specimen of female flesh Karen's mother was. She was about five foot nine, and around one hundred and thirty pounds, and well put together. She had a head full of of beautiful auburn hair like her daughter. He wondered why she was not married.

"Ralph is having a hard time keeping his eyes off of you," Karen said, noticing his intense attention to her. Her mother simply smiled.

"I can see where she gets her good looks from."

"Flattery will get you everywhere," Karen's mother responded.

"Mom raised me like she did, because of an extremely painful break up with my dad about three years ago before she remarried. He cheated on her with his secretary."

"Man, that's hard to believe. I'm not condeming your dad, but he must have been nuts."

Karen's mother just smiled, and continued to serve them lunch.

"I like him," she said to her daughter.

Karen felt good because everything seemed to have started on a good note.

"Mom, Ralph has something that he wants to ask you."

"Mrs. Simpson, I would like your permission to marry your daughter."

This caught Karen's mother completely off guard. She hesitated for what seemed like forever before respondindg.

"This is a shock, Karen" she said wide eyed.

"I know, mom, but this is a man that I simpy cannot live without. It is the same way that you first felt about my dad when you met him."

"I know, baby. Are you one hundred percent sure that this is what you want."

"Yes."

"Then that settles the issue. As long as you are happy, and know that this is what you want, then it's all right with me me."

"But what about dad?" Karen asked.

"If it's alright with me, then your step dad will have no problem"

Karen and Ralph rejoiced hugging one another, Karen kissing her mother's cheek with tears running down her face.

"Thanks mom," she said.

After leaving Karen's mom, they immediately went to Moneros to get an engagement ring.

"Well, what do I owe this pleasure to?" Smith told them greeting them at the door. "By the way, thanks Ralph for you and the guys helping to get my jewelry back to me and capturing the missing thief.

"That's OK," Ralph said.

"What can I do for you?" he asked.

"Karen, my fiance and I, would like to buy an engagment ring."

"My,but you certainly have impeccable taste in women" Smith said, giving Karen the once over.

"Thank you, Mr, Smith. I appreciate your kindness."

Karen simply smiled.

After discussinf the price range and the type of diamond that would fit their budget, they bought their first ring together

"This now makes it official," Smith said.

After leaving his office, they couldn't wait to get to Ralph's apartment to have sex for the very first time. Now that they were engaged to be married, this helped to alleviate some of the guilt about having sex out of wedlock.

"It's not as though we're just having sex for recreation, like many couples do without any plans for the future." Jeremy said."our intentions are honorable and honest, and I believe they are for the right reasons. this is where the sanctity of sex is crucial in my opinion. It is supposed to be a blissful and wonderful union between a man and a woman, and is not to be taken lightly. I remember what I was told about sex when I was very young, that no one buys a pair of shoes without trying them on first,"

"Of course you do realize that what you said in the beginning is more like the truth, and what you were told about the shoes was just an attempt to justify sex before marriage."

"I know that now, but as as a kid, I took the shoe thing at face value because it seemed to make sense."

During the course of their conversation, Jeremy's pants showed what he was feeling as a huge bulge in the crotch of his pants revealed his feelings. He was sexually charged and needed to experience sexual release. Karen felt the effects of their conversation as well, and was painfully aware of her own sexual arousal, as she looked at the evidence of Ralph's feelings visible in his pants. She too was trembling with sexual desire.

Jeremy slowly began to unbutton Karen's blouse, revealing large and succulent breasts that judded out when release from their confines, and containing large and hard brown nipples once fully visible. Karen moaned with wanton desire, as he began to circle them with his tongue, and nibble lightly on them with his mouth. Her panties were drenched with the fluid of her desire, as though they were being washed. Jeremy could not believe how wet she was as he inserted his fingers into her womanhood.

They shared the bliss of their very first sexual encounter, as well as the trauma that came with the blood from Karen at the loss of her virginity. This bothered Jeremy immensely.

"Don't let that bother you," Karen told him,"Mom already told me that it would happen with my first experience."

This made Ralph feel a lot better about everything. They layed together for several minutes afterwards, feeling as close as two people could feel for each other. They both knew that they had made the right decision.

For the next several weeks, James and John were extremely occupied with planning activities for the celebration of Jeremy and Beth's new baby, as well as the marriage ceremony of Ralph and Karen. Both events were widely publicized and notorized. The public response was overwhelming.

It is early on this Saturday fall morning, and the whether is absolutely perfect as Toby and Peg sat on the balcony of their apartment enjoying a hot cup of coffee, while listening to the melody of birds singing, and just enjoying this rare time together with nothing pressing. The office was closed, and Peg had finished her grocery shopping and house cleaning for the day. A cool fall breeze gently played with their hair and carressed their faces.This had all the makings of an easy laid back day.

"Honey, why don't we take some time today and go to the hospital snd see Jeremy and Beth's new baby?" Peg asked.

"I think that's an excellent idea," Toby responded. "Before we do though, I want to enjoy this time we're having right now. We haven't had many of them."

"Yes, this is fantastic. Do you want me to fix some breakfast?"

"Not really, this coffee is all that I need right now."

"It's been almost six months now for us here in New York, and I'm beginning to feel comfortable adjusting to big city life. Still I miss the quiet life of Midway."

"So do I at times. When all of this business with the trial is over, I think that it would be a good idea to visit Midway again and take Jeremy and Beth with us so that her mother can see her new grandson" Toby suggested.

"That's a wonderful idea. I'm also going to begin to get busy with the girls planning the wedding for Ralph and Karen."

"You see what I mean about enjoying this brief, quiet time together?"

Peg nodded her head in agreement, and reached over to take her husband's hand in hers. These are the kinds of moments that led to the births of our children she teased him.

"Yeah, they do leave enough time to get things started," he said getting her drift.

"The girls you're referring to, are they the same ones that helped you get everything started when we first arrived.?"

"Yes, the same ones. I enjoy their company."

"Man, the business at the office has doubled since the pre trial of Spaulding. I can barely keep up with the workload. Being the only private investigation agency in the area has its advantages."

"Well, it sure seems like you will have no problem with job security."

"That's for sure."

"Have you heard anything about the jury trial yet."

"No, not yet. I'm just waiting to hear from Bob about the judge's decision to pick a starting date for it to begin."

"You and the boys did a fantastic job with the investigation. I was really impressed."

Toby smiled. He always enjoyed getting affirmation about his work from Peg.

They continued to share this kind of idle, but relaxed chatter, as they took in the bliss of this time. Toby was able to breathe again without the pressures of a busy day at the office, and the regular meetings with his crew about the recovery work of the missing ruby.

Peg stood up, and told Toby that she was going to get ready and dress to go the hospital.

"Me too," Toby replied. "I enjoyed our time together like this" he finished, as he strode toward the kitchen door. About a half an hour later, they were both dressed and ready to leave. After climbing into their car, Peg asked Toby what the name of the baby was.

"I don't know. We'll just have to ask Beth when we go to her room."

When they entered the hspital they proceeded to go to the information desk.

"Beth McCallister's room please.

"She's in room 104."

"Thanks."

They both went down the corridor to Beth's room. The door was closed, and Peg told Toby that on the the maternity floor, sometimes the mothers are breast feeding. She knocked softly on the door and called Beth's name. When Beth answered, Peg told her who they were.

"Oh yes, please come in" she said.

When they entered the room, it was obvious that Beth had just finished feeding the baby.

"Don't worry, it's nothing that Toby hasn't seen before."

They all laughed together.

"Toby and I were wondering what the baby's name is?" Peg asked, as Beth craddled the baby in her arms kissing him.

"We decided to name him Terrence."

"ooh! I like that," Peg uttered.

"Terrence McCutchin. The girls will be standing in line with a name like that" Toby joked. They all thought that was funny and laughed together.

Baby Terrence was a beautiful boy with a thick crop of auburn hair, and a round face with pug nose. His eyes were a gliistening blue like his mother's, and a stern jaw like his father's. He was strikingly handsome in a pudgy kind of way.

"Your mother is going to love this baby, I assure you!" Peg exclaimed.

Toby watched and observed the bonding that happened between the two women with the baby. Things were just different when women talk about babies than it is with men. It must be the maternal instinct that women are born with that men just don't have, but doesn't mean that they care more than men do, but just in a different way. Women are women, and men are men. It's just the way that God made them.

CHAPTER SIX

THE JURY SELECTION HAS BEEN made, Read the front page of all the newspapers in the bronx .The trial by Grand Jury was set to begin in two weeks. That was the news that all of the city was waiting to reeceive, including Toby and his crew, along with Bob and the police department. They all waited patiently for word from Dale, which came a day later.

At long last the day finally arrived. There was standing room only when the doors of the courthouse opened. People had lined up outside for hours to ensure that they would get a seat. Newspaper reporters were the first to be let into the building after showing theircredentials to security. The room filled quickly, and security had to rurn away at least fifty people.

The bailiff had all the people stand in silence when judge Terrence McGill entered the room. After he took his seat, the people sat down and the trial got underway.

"There will be no flash bulbs, please, during these proceedings."

All of the reporters present nodded their approval.

"Are the dendants present?"

"Yes, your honor" Mark Blunden answered.

"Then Attorney Forsyth, you may now begin."

"Thank you, your honor. Ladies and gentlemen of the jury, we are here today primarily to determine the culpability of one, Mr. Hank Spaulding, in connection with the crime of the other defendants here. We will show to your satisafaction his involvement."

Turning directly to face Spaulding, Dale calls him to the witness stand. As he walked confidently to the stand, he gave his sister Brenda a wink and a faint smile. After taking his seat, Dale began his questioniing after first going to the podium and retreiving the ruby that was placed there.

"Mr. Spaulding, this is **exhibit** A. have you ever seen this ruby before?" he asked him, holding it up in plain sight.

"Of course I have. The police have already taken it from me."

"Did you steal it?"

"Objection" cried Mark. "That question makes no sense."

"Objection overruled. Continue"

"I'll repeat the question. Did you steal this ruby?"

"No"

"I think you're lying" Dale told him

"Objection, your honor. Counsel is badgering the witness."

"Objection is sustained. Watch it Foesyth."

"I apologize your honor. I have no further questions at this time. The witness is excused."

As Hank strode briskly back to his seat, Dale was satisified that he made his point with the jury.

"I now call Mr. Cameron to the stand."

A medium height, but portly man in his fifties, stood up and began to walk to the witness stand.

After being seated, Dale went through the exact same routine with him that he did with Spaulding.

"I called you forward because you are the self proclaimed leader of these men. Is that not right?"

"That's what they say."

"Please tell the court precisely what happened the night of the robbery."

"Jake, there" he said pointing to one of the thieves, "lowered himself down into the store from the ventilation shaft, and disarmed the outside alarm system, so that the others could enter the building from the outside undetected, once the sytem was shut down.

"Then what happened?"

"When they all came inside, the door was closed. I was the only on who had a flashlight, and I shone it on all of the jeweley cases, and told the men to pick a case that appealed to them, because it would be the one that they would clean out. There was so much jewelry in each case that I was overwhelmed. Peridots, turquose, topaz, emeralds, diamonds, you name it and it was there."

"Did you see this ruby?"

"Not really. I did catch a glimpse of somethin red, though, but I didn't pay it much attention."

"Then what happened?"

"I turned off my light and we smoked while I gave them their instructions."

"Which were?"

"That we would only have a minute or two at the most, to clean out our cases and get out of the building before the police arrived."

"And then what?"

I went to the front door and blinked my light at the get-a-way driver parked in the alley with his lights off, and signalled for him to meet us at the front door."

"And that driver was who?"

"Hank Spaulding."

Low murmers could be heard throughout the couurtroom.

"Then what happened next?"

"We broke open the cases and each guy skimmed all of the jewelry into their bags, and we beat it out of there, climbed into the car and we drove about a block down the street and parked there with our lights out, until the police responding to the alarms passed us by. Then we headed for the shack to split up the loot and wait a while until things cooled off.'

"Is there anything else you'd like to add?"

"No sir."

"Thank you, you've been a big help. You may step down."

Dale then called all of the other defendants to the stand one at a time, and repeated the same question to each one. Each one of them gave the same answer as Cameron did, except one.

"Sir, I have something else I want to add." One said.

"Take your time and say anything you'd likie to."

"Well, I notice that while we all sat around smoking and drinking, that Hank sat directly behind us just watching."

"He didn't take any of the loot?"

"No sir. He said that since he didn't help us steal it, that he didn't deserve any of it."

"That was mighty white of him" Dale said sarcasticly. Continue."

"Well, he sat there until he got up to go to his car to get his cigars."

"That was the only time he left the room?"

"Yes."

"And how long was he gone?"

"For about four or five minutes. I wondered why it took that long for him to just go and get cigars"

"Then what?"

"When he came back, he acted a little different."

"Like what?"

"Well, instead of sitting right behind us like he was, he went over and sat in a chair in the corner of the room."

"Why do you think that was?"

"I asked him, and he said that he didn't want his cigar smoke to bother us. With all of the smoking that we were doing, nobody would have even noticed. I thought that was a little odd."

"I agree. Anything else you want to add?"

"No sir."

"Good you've been very helpful also. Thank you. you're dismissed."

After the man left the witness stand, Dale spoke to the judge.

"Your honor, may I have permission to approach the bench?"

"You may. Blunden do you have any objections?"

"No your honor."

With that, Dale went to the bench before the judge for a side bar, and whispered to him in a hushed voice.

"Sir, I'd like to ask for a fifteen minute recess in order to review my notes."

"I see no problem with that. Your request is granted."

Dale thanked the judge and returned to his seat.

"There will be a fifteen minute recess. Take the time to get a cup of coffee or a snack before returning." The judge ordered.

With that, the proceedings came to a halt. The room emptied out noisily as people scurried to the refreshment center. Bob and Toby remained in the room talking.

"What do you think this recess is about?" Toby asked him.

"I don't know," confessed Bob," but I do know Dale. He's up to something, but I have no clue what it is."

When the judge came back into the courtroom and took his seat at the bench, the trial was resumed. Dale recalled Spaulding to the witness stand. After retrieving the ruby from the podium, he held it up in plain sight, and again asked Spaulding the same question as he did before.

"Did you steal this ruby? Remember you are under oath."

"No."

"Then how did you come to be in possession of it?"

"Objection your honor. Counsel is being redundant. he has already answered this question.'

"Counsel?"

"Your honor, this line of questioning is pertenent to drawing my conclusion."

"Objection overruled. Please continue"

"Thank you sir. How did you get this ruby in your possession?"

"I found it."

"That's not exactly true is it, Mr. Spaulding?"

Hank immediately became very fidgety and nervous, and began to sweat profusely.

"How many times do I have to answer this question?" Hank shouted irritated and angry.

"Until you tell us the whole truth. You know that you did not just haphazardly stumble across it, don't you. tell us the truth Spaulding." Dale demanded.

"What do you want me to say? I already have. I've told you several times that I found it." Spaulding spat out wide eyed, but visibly frustrated and shaken.

"But **how** did you find it? under what circumstances? You know that you found it **after** knowing that it had been stolen by your buddies, didn't you. admit it Spaulding! we just want to know the truth."

"Objection, your honor. Counsel is again leading the witness."

"Attorney Forsyth exactly where is this line of questioning leading to?"

"Your honor, what I intend to prove is that the defendant is telling a half truth, and a half truth is still a lie."

"What do you mean by a half truth?" demanded Mark.

"It's true that he passed a lie detector test days ago, saying that he found the ruby, but didn't steal it. but he was only referring to the robbery of the jewelry store itself, which he did not participate in as a thief. However, he did, nonetheless, steal it."

"What makes you arrive at that conclusion?" Mark demanded.

"Because he stole it from his buddies his buddies bye proxy, when he went to his car while everybody else was busy dividing up the loot."

"How do you figure?" Mark asked.

"He was gone far too long to just have gone to his car to get his cigars. You heard the other witness say that yourself. and then when he came back into the room, he sat over in a corner by himself, away from everybody else. it was not because of the cigar smoke, was it Spaulding? it was because of something else, wasn't it? " Dale argued, looking directly at Spaulding.

"Something else like what?" Mark demanded to know.

"He knows what I mean. He sat over by himself because he now had the ruby in his jacket pocket which he found on the ground outside of the shack."

"That's total speculation and guess work, and you know it" barked Dale.

"Oh, yeah? Let's just see. I recall Spaulding to the witness stand.

Hank got up from his seat and retook the witness stand.

"Now, Mr. Spaulding, tell the court exactly why you changed your seat when you came back from your car. It wasn't just because of your cigar smoke, was it?"

"You tell me" Spaulding replied.

"It was because you were now feeling guilty, and a little insecure, because of the ruby in your jacket pocket that ypu found outside going to your car. Isn't that right, Spaulding." Dale said accusingly

"That's what you say" Spaulding shot back.

"We know that you did not take any of the loot that was divided up, so you couldn't have picked up the ruby from off the table, yet you had it, and took it home with you after the group broke up. isn't that right?"

Spaulding just sat staring straight ahead, but sayng nothing.

"You stole the ruby from the others, bye proxy, when you found it going to your car to get your cigars. that makes you an accessory after the fact,and equally as guilty as the others."

Dale was more than satisfied that he had gotten his point across to the court, and now turned to face the jury.

"Ladies and gentlemen of the jury, we now know the truth of how Mr. Spaulding came to have the missing ruby, that none of the others knew anything about. He didn't just find it, he stole it when the theives were in the shack after the robbery. This is why he tried to plead the fifth earlier, when asked about the location of where he supposedly found the ruby. He knew that this was the clue that the Reliford private investigators were looking for. Your honor, the prosecution rests."

Commotion had to be quelched by the judge at the conclusion of Dale's presentaton.

"The jury is now directed to retire to your chamber until you reach a verdict."

Pandemonium reigned in the courthouse room. High fives were exchanged throughout the room, and congratulatory hugs were given everywhere. It was universally believed by those present at the time, that the verdict was a foregone conclusion.

Toby, Bob, and all of the investigators embraced one another, and all congratulated Dale on his experise.

"You were fantastic again" Bob told him. "I warned them about how you operate, when they were worried and concerened about how things would turn out."

"Well, it's not over yet,"Dale cautioned them. "The jury still has to render their decision."

"Ah, that's a done deal," Toby volunteered.

"I hope your'e right."

"Count on it," Bob added.

As people lingered in the courthouse awaiting the verdict, they drank coffee and ate snacks as conversation continued steadily. Brenda was comforted by Ralph as they waited. Eventhough the outcome was inevitable, it was still her brother's life that was hanging in the blance. She sat with her eyes filled with tears.

It took the jury only one hour to render their verdict.

"Has the jury reached a verdict?" judge McGill asked when the trial reconvened.

"Yes, we have your honor. We find all of the defendants guilty of all charges."

Bedlam broke out all across the courtroom. It took the bailiffs and security ten minutes to restore order, in order to hear the judge's final disposition.

"Sentencing will be done next month. Court is adjourned.

Needlesss to say, the entire city became unglued. The news media had a field day. Toby and his investigators were again the talk of the day. They were feted every where they went. Toby called them all together in their office.

"It looks like this will probably be our last time together, unless something similar like this comes up again. I'm settled into my office, business is great, and Peg and I will probably begin to look for our own house. All of you will go back to work just like you were before I came and monsero's hired us. It has been a fantastic journey, and you guys have been great."

"Well, all good things must end, so the saying goes." Jeremy commented.

"It brings to mind the song Don Merideth used to sing on Monday night football; 'turn out the light, the party's over'" said Ralph.

There were sad faces everywhere in the room.

"Perk up, fellas. if I ever need you again all I have to do is just call. This not goodbye, just I'll see you later." Toby said, trying to lift their spirits. It seemed to have had some effect. The boys begin to shake hands, smile, and pat each other on the back. Toby smiled. This was sort of like his family, he mused. After the group had wrapped up their farewell, and Toby was left alone in his office, he picked up his phoneand called Bob.

"Bob, Toby here" he said when Bob answered. "How's it going?"

"Hey, Toby. Couldn't be better. I've even gotten a small raise!"

"Ah, hah! You deserve it."

"Thanks. What's up?" Bob asked.

"You and I need to talk with Smith at Monseros about the plan to take the ruby to Cairo."

"Yes, you're right. when do you want to do it?"

"How about tomorrow morning?"

"Sounds good to me?" Bob told him.

"I'll call him right away and arrange the meeting."

"Good. Just let me know the time."

Toby immediately called Smith to arrange the meeting.

"Why do I need to meet with the police?" Smith wanted to know.

"It's OK., there's nothing to be concerned about. We can talk about it in the morning"

"How about nine thirty or so?"

"Good. I'll call Bob and let him know."

After calling Bob, Toby leaned back in his chair, and continued to enjoy smoking his pipe and relaxing. All that needed to be done now about the case, was to wait for the judge to pass sentence on the criminals. This feeling of euphoria lasted all the way home.

"Peg, I think it's time for you to get with the girls, and begin house hunting for us."

"I was just waiting for you to tell me that."

"I think it's time. I just got a raise, not that I really needed it for us to start, but it does come in handy. We need to have our own place."

"I was a little reluctant at first to come up here, but this has worked out far better than I ever imagined it would" Peg beamed.

Toby just smiled. He loved to see Peg happy and enthusiastic like this.

"Mr. Smith, Bob from police headquarters" Toby said as he introduced Smith to him.

"Pleased to meet you" Smith responded. "come in. would you like a cup of coffee?"

"That's the best news I've heard this morning" Bob answered.

After they were all seated, Toby began the conversation.

"Bob and I wanted to talk with you about your ruby that was recovered."

"What about it?"

"I hate to tell you this, but you will probably never see it again."

"Why not?" Smith asked incredulously.

"The police discovered that a huge robbery took place in Cairo, Egypt involoving a stolen heirloom from a diamond cutter there, and believe your ruby may be a part of the missing whole piece. The police want to take it to Cairo and make it a part of their investigation."

"But why will I not get it back when they finish with it?"

"They want to return to its rightful owner."

"I paid twenty thousand dollars for that ruby, where does that leave me?"

"I know" Toby said sympathetically, "We are going to try and get your money back from the guy you bought it from."

"How will you do that?"

"Oh, we have our ways" Bob replied.

"I still have the man's name, address, and phone number that you gave me previously" Toby said handing it to Bob.

"Hmm, a Mr. Ruben Cresswell" murmured Bob. "the name sounds vaguely familiar. how and where did you get it from him?" Bob asked.

Smith told Bob the same set of circimstanes around him getting the ruby that he told Toby earlier.

Bob nodded his head.

"I can understand why you were so careless in getting the ruby, and why you chose to ignore all of the red flags popping up everywhere. we'll do everything we can to at least get your money back.'

Smith thanked them both as they left, and headed back to Bob's office.

"I really feel sorry for him" Bob said. "he seems like such a nice and honest man."

"I know. I felt the same way."

"What I plan to do is to send Dick, and one of my detectives with him to Cairo. I don't want Dick traveling by himself with such an expensive Gem."

Toby remembered Dick well from the investigation that took place in Midway over a year ago, when Rod and jeremy were on trial for their lives. In order not to raise suspicion from the town folk about an investigation by outside authorities, they chose instead to bring in investigators undercover, the ages of Rod and Jeremy to do the work. They were all classmates at Wayne State and in their senior year, with Ralph doing the forensic work, majoring in microbiology, and Dick handling the investigation majoring in criminology.

Dick Wingate was about six feet tall, and weighed 175 pounds with a solidly built frame, at around twenty five years of age, and still single with a beautiful red haired girlfriend, who had recently graduated from Wayne State herself. Dick had blonde hair and was clean shaven with a freshly scrubbed face and looks like a choir or altar boy. His boyish face, however was stern looking, and he was full of self confidence.

"I think that's an outstanding master plan" Smith observed. "I just have to get used to the idea of never seeing my ruby again. But it will be tremendous help to get my twenty thousands dollars back, if you are able to do that."

"Well, that will put you back to square one at least" Toby remarked.

"That'll be a relief in itself. guaranteed." Smith acknowledged.

Bob stood up and shook Smith's hand firmly before they left. Back at Bob's office, the two continued talking for a while.

"At this pont, the only thing that needs to happen before Dick takes the ruby to Cairo, is to wait for judge McGill to pass sentence on the thieves. When that is done, the book can officially be closed on the case, and we will then be able to take the ruby out of the country."

"Has Dale contacted you at all?"

"Not yet, but he will just as soon as he hears from the judge."

That news came down a week later after their meeting. Bob called Toby's office to give him the news.

"The judge sentenced all them, including Spaulding fifteen to twenty years on all counts."

"Hallelulujah!" Toby yelled. "Finally, finally, it's all over."

Bob enthusiastically shared shared his celebration.

"Now we can get down to serious business." He concluded.

Bob called Dick and one of his sergeants, kevin Jarvis into the office to make their final plans for the trip.

"I am giving Dick the ruby to take with the two of you the to Cairo. Don't say anything about it to anyone until you talk to Clayton Turnbull, the man who sold the ruby to Mr. Smith."

CHAPTER SEVEN

CAIRO

SERGEANT GIVENS WAS A LARGE man in his fifties, bald, and witrh a handsome,but rugged face. He wieghed 165 pounds, and stood six feet six inches tall. 'What a body guard' Dick thought to himsel as he observed him. As they boarded the plane for their flight to Egypt, it was the first international flight of Dick's life, and he was a little apprehensive and nervous to say the least. They were seated in first class with plenty of room.

Dick settled down in his seat, closed his eyes, and tried to relax with little success. The sergeant settled in and appeared perfectly at ease.

"Kevin, I can tell that you are comfortable with flying."

"I love it."

"Don't you ever feel insecure and powerless when you're up in the air, and completely out of control?"

"Not really, I just don't think about it."

"But how can you just block it out like that? When I ride on something, I want to have the power to get off of it when I want to. You lose that control when you fly."

"But how much control do you really have when you drive? You can't control what the driver in the other lane does, only a foot or so away."

"Well, I never thought of it like that before," Dick confessed.

Kevin smiled as Dick talked about flying. He had heard this kind of conversation before from folk nervous about flying.

"Kevin, how long have you been on the force?" Dick asked him.

"About five years. I remember when you first came aboard. Everybody was talking about how you turned down the job with the FBI to go to work with us."

"That was a no brainer when I learned that my classmates, Rod and Jeremy, had agreed to work with their dads at the corporate headquarters of the enterprise."

"I would guess that you may probably be up for a promotion after this over."

"Who knows. Maybe."

"Well, anyway, I feel good that you're with me."

After fastening his seat belt at the instructions of the stewardess, Dick waitied for take off. A few minutes into the flight, a movie came on for the passengers on a big overhead screen, which Dick was not interested in. He noticed how many of the other passengers had their eyes glued to the screen, while others sat looking out the windows. Kevin simply settled back, closed his eyes and waited.

To Dick's surprise and delight, a beautiful stewardess came down the center of the aisle with a tray she was pushing, loaded down with refreshments, including alcoholic beverages.

"Would you like anything?" she purred.

"Yes, what kind f drinks do you have with alcohol?"

She mentioned several, and Dick settled for a rum and coke, while sergeant Givens wanted a manhattan. Dick had decided that the alcohol would help him relax until he fell asleep. He had a drink, each time the stewardess came down the aisle, trying in vain to get him to eat peanuts and other snacks. After downing several drinks, he finally fell asleep listening to sound of the jet engines. He slept until he heard the voice of the pilot announcing that they would be landing in Cairo in twenty minutes, and to make sure that their seat belts were fastened.

As they descended, Dick was painfully aware that he had heard that this was the most crucial part of flying; the take off and the landing. He realized that they were completely at the mercy of God to make a safe landing. There was no conversation coming from any of the other passengers, as they all looked out of their windows or had their heads buried in their books. They were all having similar thoughts. When the plane finally touched down, conversation erupted from the passangers, as words of thanksgiving were shared among them.

The terminal was bristling with activity as passengers made their way down the corridors to the baggage claim area, and to gates where they would be picked up.

"This is the part I don't like" confessed Kevin as they made their to the baggage claim section.

Dick did not care for all of the turmoil that existed too, and felt better knowing that Kevin didn't didn't like it either. After claiming their baggage, which seemed to take forevert, they headed to the gate where they were to be picked up.

Standing in one of the aisles, there was a man holding up a sign for Dick Wingate. That was their pick up man.

"Dick Wingate?" he asked as they appeoached him.

"Yes, this is me and sergeant Givens." He said as the two of them showed their ID's.

Once outside, they were escorted to a plain vehicle with two other men inside.

"Welcome to Cairo, gentlemen" they were greeted.

"Thank you," Dick said.

When they arrived at the Police headquarters, Dick was surpised to see how similar it was to their own.

'We are here from the NYPD to verify that an Heirloom ruby was stolen here over a month ago." Dick said as they both showed their ID's.

:That's right" said a well dressed man. "Your chief told us that you were coming." I'm captain Peredes, of the Cairo police force.

"We have the ruby from New York that was stolen from one of our jewelry stores in the Bronx, and we were wondering if it could connected with the robbery that you had here."

"That's a good possibility. May I see it please." The captain asked them.

Dick opened up the locked briefcase that he had at his side, and retrieved the ruby from inside. The captain looked it over carefully before handing it back.

"This certainly looks like it could b a part of the big one that was stolen. The complete stone was estimated at over 15 million Amerian dollars."

"Whew" whistled Kevin.

"How's that investigation going?"Dick asked the captain.

"Not so great" the captain aswered. "We are still trying to find out where the diamond came from before it was stolen from the cutters."

"What makes you think that this is a part of the stolen Heirloom?" Dick asked him.

"We can tell because it has been cut from a larger piece. Our expert gemologist told us what to look for."

"Will having it help you?" Dick asked.

"I don't know, but it certainly can't hurt" the captain asked.

"So, you have very little clues at this point" Kevin asked.

"That's right, but every little bit helps."

"I don't feel comfortable walking around with this ruby. I'd prefer to leave it here with your department." Dick said.

"Thank you. it certainly is a beautiful piece. I can imagine what the rest of it would look like. We'll certainly be in touch with you as we progress with our investigation."

"Thank you," Dick said.

"Can you give us a map to the city that we can use to visit some of the sights here?" Kevin asked.

"That's a piece of cake" the captain replied.

After getting the information that kevin had requested, the captain concluded their didcussion.

"My men will escort you to your hotel."

"Thank you.

Once they arrived and checked into their hotel, Kevin and Dick continued their conversation.

"I want to see the city tomorrow before we meet with Mr. Clayton Turnbull." Dick said.

"Sounds like a good idea" Kevin agreed.The hotel was very ritzy and very expensive. Their room had two kingsized beds, complete with a kitchen and refrigerator with wet bar.

"That's what I was looking for," Dick remarked when he opened up the fridge.

"You know that you have to pay for everything you drink. They take a complete inventory of everything in there." Kevin said.

"Yeah, it figures. They don't miss a trick."

Both men chuckled at Kevin's remark as they helped themselves to the ice, and drinks in the fridge, they looked over the map of Cairo given to them, and decided what sights they would see in the morning. After a while, they took turns taking showers, and then turned in for a much needed sleep. Their day was more exhausting than they had noticed.

Early the next morning, they discovered that they were starving. Kevin called down to the office and ordered a breakfast be sent up to their room. They had eggs, bacon and sausage, complete with toast and a pitcher of coffee. Dick thought to himself that he could really get used to this.

"I can tell this is your first experience with special assignments like this." Kevin said, as he observed Dick's wide eyed excitement.

"Wow, this something else" Dick responded.

"I was on the force about three years before you joined us, and you remind me of the very first time that I was put on special assignment. This won't be your last time, though, because Bob really likes you. you'll go a long way."

After eating and getting dressed, left to see the town after renting a car from a local dealer near by. They decided that their first stop was to go and see the Egyptian antiques at the musium downtown.

Printed in the United States
By Bookmasters